MARIAH'S REVENGE

(Sequel to Hunting Mariah)

I0563297

J.E. SPINA

PUBLISHED BY J.E. SPINA

COPYRIGHT 2018 JANICE SPINA & J.E. SPINA

COVER BY JOHN SPINA

ALL RIGHTS RESERVED

Names, characters, places and events are products of this author's imagination.

DEDICATION

To my husband, John Spina, for all his support and encouragement and the dinners he cooked so I could continue to write

ACKNOWLEDGEMENTS

A very special thank you to my wonderful beta readers, Patricia Bradley, Sandra J. Jackson, Michele Rolfe, and my content editor, John Spina, for working tirelessly to read and review my work and for their helpful input. Their assistance is appreciated.

OTHER BOOKS BY J.E. SPINA

Hunting Mariah (Book 1 –
mystery/suspense/serial crime)

How Far is Heaven
(paranormal/romance/mystery)

An Angel Among Us (A Short Story
Collection – multi-genres)

BOOKS BY JANICE SPINA

<u>Pre-School to Grade Three:</u>

Louey the Lazy Elephant

Ricky the Rambunctious Raccoon

Jerry the Crabby Crayfish (won Pinnacle Book Achievement Award)

*Lamby the Lonely Lamby (*Received Silver Medal from Mom's Choice Awards)

Jesse the Precocious Polar Bear

Broose the Moose on the Loose (Won Pinnacle Book Achievement Award)

Sebastian Meets Marvin the Monkey

Colby the Courageous Cat

Jeffrey the Jittery Giraffe

Clarence Henry the Hermit Crab

Middle-Grade/Preteen/YA Books:

Davey & Derek Junior Detectives, Book 1, The Case of the Missing Cell Phone

(Won Pinnacle Book Achievement Award & HM Reader's Favorite)

Davey & Derek Junior Detectives Series Book 2, The Case of the Mysterious Black Cat (Won Pinnacle Book Achievement Award)

Davey & Derek Junior Detectives, Book 3, The Case of the Magical Ivory Elephant (Won Pinnacle Book Achievement Award & Reader's Favorite Silver Medal)

The Case of the Brown Scraggly Dog (Davey & Derek Junior Detectives Series Book 4)

The Case of the Sad Mischievous Ghost (Davey & Derek Junior Detectives Series, Book 5) (Won Silver Medal from Authorsdb Cover Contest and a Pinnacle Book Achievement Award)

Table of Contents

CHAPTER ONE

Sage moved quickly through the wooded areas well beyond the hospital. He hadn't been able to get to his intended targets but he did manage to save his own life by killing the agents. Sage remembered the sound of one agent's neck as it broke and the other agent's nose as it collapsed into his brain after he had delivered a palm heel strike directly to the agent's face.

He planned to hide away for a while until he could make plans to complete the job he needed to do. His father had often told him about a group of summer cabins that were unused in the winter on Tambor Lake. Many years he asked his father to take him for a vacation but they never got there. His father was always too busy dealing with the dead bodies and their families at his funeral home.

Sage had enjoyed preparing the bodies for burial as his father had taught him as early as eight years old. What his father didn't know was that Sage also added his own special touches, carvings and mutilations on the bodies in places where his father wouldn't easily be able to detect.

It had all ended when Sage turned sixteen. On this day his father walked in on him as he was carving a woman's body on her back. That day his father had a massive heart attack that claimed his life.

Sage was committed to a psychiatric hospital after he became uncontrollable following his father's death. His mother feared for her life around him.

In time, Sage managed to escape. He had a plan to hide away but not before retrieving some money his father had hidden in one of the vaults where the bodies were stored in his funeral home. Sage's father tendency to forget to bring the money to the bank after funerals, would come in handy when he had to find a place to hunker down.

That's when it all had started for Sage – the murders, all the blood, and the feeling of being alive for the first time in his sixteen years. He began his killing spree a few years after he ran away. The body count had spread across three states, New Hampshire, Vermont, and New York.

He looked forward to more killings as soon as he could possibly find some victims. Maybe he would get lucky at the lake and find some helpless soul there to practice on. He planned to come back to kill his brother and niece one day when the heat was off him. It could take up to a year, maybe more, but he was patient when it came to doing things right. His brother and niece wouldn't escape him this time. He would make sure of it. He would not give up his chance to seek revenge from his family for abandoning him.

***

Sage stopped abruptly when he saw some houses ahead. The darkening sky offered some cover, but not enough. He settled down in the bushes and watched for any movement in or around the closest house. There were a few lights on but no signs of life.

He knew he couldn't wait long. The police would be looking for him. He was a murderer at large, a fact he considered amusing. He didn't think of himself as a murderer but merely an artist practicing his craft, and he definitely enjoyed mastering his artistry. He smiled and stood as he saw an old woman letting a dog out.

The woman was quite elderly and hobbled back inside with a limp holding her lower back. Sage suspected she was in her late eighties or more. At least she wouldn't be a threat to him with the dog outside. He decided to move forward and get to her door quickly. If the dog came after him he would deliver a round kick to his chops to silence him.

He walked toward the house and looked around for the dog. Evidently the dog was old and deaf because Sage could see him in the field on the side of the house but the dog never even looked his way.

Sage raced up the walk and knocked on the door. He waited several minutes and then heard a soft voice calling out, "Hold on a minute."

The old woman looked even older close up as she peered through her screen door at Sage. She squinted at him and leaned closer to the screen.

"Who are you? What do you want?" she asked shakily as she held onto the doorknob keeping the door closed between them.

Sage laughed at the fact that it would take a lot more than a flimsy screen door to keep him out. "I'm here to find a place to stay. Do you have a room I can rent?"

"No, I don't. Now go away!"

"Oh, that's not the answer I wanted to hear," Sage chortled, looking forward to taking out this ornery old woman. It wouldn't be challenging but could be fun anyway. She appeared to be feisty in spite of her age, similar to his adopted mother.

Sage grabbed and yanked the door handle. The woman lost her balance and fell forward onto the front porch. He pulled her up and dragged her back into the house.

The dog's ears perked up. He barked and ran toward the house. He squinted his eyes and his ears pulled back tight against his head as he sensed that his mistress was in distress.

Sage slammed the door shut keeping the dog out and pushed the woman onto her couch. The woman rubbed her back and elbow where she had fallen and noticed blood dripping down her arm. She used her apron to wipe away the blood while keeping her rheumy eyes on Sage.

***

Detectives Kim Snyder and Chris Armano were finished up with their investigation and getting ready to leave the Darien J. Roberts Psychiatric Hospital. They waited while Dan, the Lobby

Attendant, unlocked the door. The detectives were busy with their usual banter when they both stopped short. What the detectives saw out in the parking lot was beyond belief.

CHAPTER TWO

Mariah and her family were at The Windy Port Restaurant for a celebratory dinner. She looked around at her family, smiled, and with a huge sigh of relief she thanked God for all of them.

Mariah's family were oblivious of her silent observation of them. They appeared happy in spite of what they had gone through earlier in the day. Mariah shivered when she started to relive some of her nightmare but shook it off when her boyfriend, Tony, grasped her hand, squeezed it, and brought it to his lips.

"Mariah, are you all right, honey?"

"Oh…yeah, I'm great! I was thinking…but it's in the past. He can't harm any of us anymore."

"No, he can't! You've got this, Mariah." Tony kissed her hand again. He changed the subject. "Aren't you going back to school?"

"Well, I guess I should now. I have a lot to do and I plan to write the great American novel," Mariah laughed.

Tony leaned over, kissed Mariah's cheek, and gave her hand another squeeze.

Robert looked at his niece when he heard her delightful laugh. He smiled and relaxed for the first time since it had all begun before Mariah was born.

His brother was now in the custody of the FBI. It had taken many years and the deaths of several young women before he was caught. Robert was thankful that Mariah hadn't been one of the victims. Though Juniper, Jay, Sage or whatever his brother was going by for a name, was an unstable and dangerous man. Robert feared for his family and wouldn't rest until his brother was in prison for the rest of his life. Sage, most likely, would be committed to an insane asylum. But Robert would do all he could to insure that Sage never left that place.

"Robert, honey, please make a toast for us," Beatrice Fontana requested.

"Okay, Mother. Looking around at all of you sorry souls, only kidding. I am grateful to have you wonderful people on my side. Especially you, Mother, you were pretty tough on Sage when he got arrested. I'm glad I am the chosen son!"

"Well, if you don't do a proper toast you may not be for long!" Beatrice chuckled.

"Oops, sorry! I couldn't help it," Robert snickered, enjoying himself. "Well, okay, let's raise our glasses to Mariah for her bravery, strength, perseverance; to Tony for his courage and tremendous work in bringing things together for all of us; and to Miguel and Ronald for their quick thinking and muscles. Last but not least, to my mother and sister, for the use of their scarves to tie Sage up."

Everyone clinked glasses all around congratulating each other on the parts they played in bringing Sage to justice.

Robert's cell rang. He pulled it out of his back pocket and took a quick look at the text. What he saw made his face blanch. He called the number back and listened.

Robert finally stood and gathered everyone. They waited and observed Robert's facial expressions which were beginning to unglue them all.

Beatrice reached out and took her son's hand as she implored, "Robert, what's wrong, dear? You look like you've seen a ghost."

"I think I did, Mother. I have something to share with you, and I apologize first for what I have to say. I don't like it any more than you will."

"Oh, Robert, what is it? You are beginning to unnerve me," his mother stressed.

There is no other way to say it than right out. "Sage got away!"

"What? What did you say, Robert?" Beatrice held her hand over her heart as she gripped Robert's arm.

"How…how could he possibly get away?" his sister, Betsy, asked incredulously.

"There were two armed FBI agents on him! That's impossible!" Ronald, Beatrice's chauffeur added.

Tony wrapped his arms around Mariah who had begun to tremble. "It's okay, Mariah. You're safe with us here. We'll handle this. Please don't get upset. I won't let anyone or anything harm you. I promise."

Robert continued to explain, "Dan called to say that the detectives came back into the hospital to report that Sage had escaped after he killed two agents. The police are there with an ambulance to pick up the bodies and are checking around the premises. It looks like Sage is long gone. The police have an APB out on him and will keep the two detectives there to watch over us. They suggested we go back to the hospital and stay put until they know more. They doubt he will be back to the scene of his crime but you never can tell with Sage."

"Oh my God, Robert!" Betsy exclaimed in disbelief.

"What are we going to do?" Frank, Betsy's husband, queried as he hugged his wife.

They moved over to hug their daughter and whispered words of comfort as Mariah continued to tremble.

Mariah hugged her parents and put on a brave front as she announced, "I will not hide away from Sage, nor will I allow him to bully me and force me to cower."

"Oh my dear, you are a gem," Beatrice agreed and beamed in approval.

"You have been through so much, sweetheart," Betsy stressed, "and I don't want to see you in danger again. You need to lay low until the police catch him."

"Yes, I plan to, Mom, but I won't allow him to have the upper hand. He better watch his own back!" Mariah responded forcefully as she stood tall and composed.

Tony pulled Mariah in for a hug. "Well, well, my girl has certainly grown up. She puts the fear of God in me!" Tony teased.

"I am proud of you, Mariah, that you can face this with such aplomb and panache," her grandmother announced.

"Thank you, Gram. I'm trying my best. You have all been there for me through this trying time and now I want to give back. It's time for me to do my part."

"Of course, we know you are a young woman now, Mariah. We are proud of you and all that you have had to contend with." Robert stepped forward and hugged Mariah and kissed her forehead.

"Thank you, Uncle Robert, for all that you have done to help me get my memory back. Now we must move forward and help the police find Sage and put him away for good this time."

"Oh boy, you are right on the money, my dear," Ronald piped in with a smile.

"You are quite the muscle man, Ronald. You would make a great bouncer the way you tackled and held Sage down so he could be restrained," Mariah returned Ronald's smile.

"Well, I was an amateur boxer and a wrestler in high school. I could hold my own, that's about it."

"Really, Ronald, I didn't know that," Beatrice nodded her approval. "Now I feel extra safe in your care."

"You will always be safe in my care, dear lady!" Ronald bowed to Beatrice.

Robert interrupted the light repartee to get everyone back to the problem at hand, finding Sage. "Listen everyone, we need to get back to the hospital and hunker down and do some brainstorming with the police. They may have some idea where Sage has gone. Ronald, let's get everyone in the limo and head back now."

Robert apologized to the waiter, paid for their drinks and gave him a generous tip. "Sorry but we have an emergency and won't be staying for dinner."

The waiter nodded, took his tip and walked away.

"I'm ready. Let's go." Ronald led the way to the limo, unlocked the doors and started the engine.

As Ronald began to pull out, a police car stopped them. An officer came over to the limo and Ronald rolled down the window to find out what he wanted.

"Are you Dr. Fontana?"

Ronald shook his head and called out to the doctor, "Dr. Fontana, you are being summoned."

Robert opened his window and stuck his head out to see what was going on.

"Can I help you officer? We are on our way back to my hospital."

"Yes, that is why I'm here. I am your escort. Follow me please."

Robert rolled up the window and looked at his family and shrugged. "I guess they don't trust us to find our way back by ourselves."

"Robert, dear, I think the police are only being careful. After all, Sage could be roaming around in the woods outside the hospital waiting for a chance to get you or any of us."

"I guess you're right, Mother. Better be safe than sorry later," Robert sighed heavily.

Robert's mind was whirling with different scenarios as Ronald drove the short distance back to the hospital with the police escort. The first thing he was going to do was take out his gun from the safe and keep it on him. He wanted to be ready in case Sage came back. This time he would not talk but shoot first, no questions asked.

CHAPTER THREE

Sage dragged the old woman's body into the bathroom and wrapped her in the shower curtain to contain the blood. He calmly cleaned the front room and thoroughly washed his hands.

He was hungry and had wasted enough time dealing with her. She wasn't an easy kill. She fought until the end and spit at him. She had reached out and scratched his face when he threatened her with his knife. He had had enough of her. He had slit her throat as she had sworn at him. Somehow he felt that she had gotten the last word in. He had made sure to use bleach on her hands to remove his skin and blood from her nails.

Now he needed to get rid of her dog. It had been barking non-stop since Sage had entered the house. Sage cautiously opened the door and called the dog in. The dog barked and jumped at his leg and tried to bite him but Sage kicked it sharply in the head and broke its neck.

Sage planned to bury both bodies outside in the backyard once it was darker. If anyone questioned where the old woman and her dog were he would say that she had gone away and he was taking care of her house until she returned. He hadn't seen any of the neighbors. They evidently kept to themselves. That's the way he liked it.

Sage rummaged around in the refrigerator until he found a casserole with chicken and vegetables that was still warm and smelled quite good. He ate half of it and put the rest away for later. He needed to sustain himself for he hoped to be miles away at Tambor Lake by late evening.

He ransacked the bedroom for anything of value but all he found was some cheap jewelry. He had already pocketed the woman's wedding ring after killing her. It wasn't much but it could get him a few extra dollars.

He went through every drawer in the house and even checked the cookie, sugar, and flour canisters in case the old woman had stuffed them with some money. No luck, until he came to her recipe books. Tucked inside each book was a stash of bills, enough to keep him going for more than a month. Lucky for him the old woman didn't put it into the bank.

He would leave as soon as he possibly could, take what he could from the old woman's house, and pick up whatever else he needed at a store on the way to the lake. He looked around for keys that would indicate she had a car. He found a set of keys on the inside of a cabinet door. He snatched them up and went out to the garage.

The garage was filled with boxes and junk but under it all was an old Cadillac Eldorado with wings and all. It looked like it was in pretty good condition though. The paint was still bright blue and the wheels didn't have much wear. The inside was clean with shiny leather seats and a dust free dash board. Sage cleared the stuff away from the car and checked it out for gas. It was half full, probably enough to get him to Tambor Lake where he could get a fill up.

He went back into the house and found a few plastic bags and began to stuff them with canned goods, bread, crackers and bottled water. The old woman certainly didn't need any of it. Sage laughed out loud at his own humor.

He put the supplies in the trunk of the car and went in search of a shovel to dig the graves for the old woman and her dog. He wanted to complete this tedious job, shower, and get a move on.

Sage chose a secluded area amongst some trees in the backyard to begin digging. The six-foot high stockade fence helped to give him some cover. Hopefully when he dug he wouldn't hit too many rocks or roots from the trees to hinder his progress. After an hour of heavy digging, Sage lifted the bodies of the old woman and her dog and dumped them into the hole. He patted down the earth around them and scattered some leaves and branches to cover up his work. He was betting on no one looking back there and finding them for a long time.

He went back into the house and hastily showered. Luckily the old woman had saved some men's clothes in the closet that most likely were her husband's. He chose some to take them along with him. Sage had found a descent pair of khakis and a t-shirt that fit him along with some underwear and socks. He kept his sneakers on when he couldn't find a pair of shoes to fit. He had grabbed a jacket in case it got colder.

He was fatigued from all the digging but decided not to waste any more time. He would head out after he finished packing the car and get to the lake sooner than he originally planned. He knew the police would keep looking for him and wouldn't stop until they found him.

Sage closed up the house. Looking around him one last time, he checked to make sure he hadn't left anything of his own behind. He wiped off his knife, pocketed it along with his dirty clothes, and cleaned up the blood and his fingerprints on everything he had touched as best he could. He didn't want the police to know he had been there and had the old woman's car. Sage would choose another vehicle as soon as possible, but being farther away now would be more advantageous.

He couldn't afford to make any mistakes this time. He wanted everything to go smoothly. He would wait as long as he could to come back and finish off what he had started – killing his brother and his niece. Sage would also take out his adopted mother and his sister and her husband. He would wipe out his whole family.

As he drove along he thought over what his family would be thinking about now. He was sure they had heard about his escape. The police had most likely found the bodies of the agents out in the parking lot by now. Sage smiled and chuckled thinking over the fear they must all be feeling not knowing where he was or when he would return to kill them.

He popped open a bottle of water and chugged it. He hadn't realized how thirsty he was. Digging graves would do that to you.

Two hours later he arrived at the camp to find it closed and deserted. He chose a secluded cabin and picked the lock to gain access. He unpacked the car and brought everything into the cabin. Luckily the electricity was working and he also had water. It might get a little cold at night if the heat wasn't on but he would survive. He had learned how to do without many things in his lifetime.

Sage checked out the kitchen and found some items in the cabinets that he could use. The last tenants had left canned goods and paper products. The cabin was fully furnished and all he had to do was find the sheets to make up the bed and towels for a shower in the morning.

Sage opened up a can of beans and warmed it on the gas stove. He had brought some crackers and a loaf of bread from the old woman's house which would make a quick and easy supper.

***

Brad, the owner of the resort, arrived back at the cabins with some supplies. He looked out at the farthest cabin tucked in the wooded area and noticed the lights on. He wasn't expecting any visitors until early morning. He put away all his supplies. He would stock all the cabins for the incoming visitors later. Who could be out there now? The owner/manager walked toward the cabin to find out.

As he got closer he noticed the old Caddy sitting in front. He knocked on the door and tried the lock. It opened and he walked in. The lights suddenly went out.

CHAPTER FOUR

Detectives Armano and Snyder went back into the hospital. They were still in shock over what they had found. When Detective Armano had spoken with Captain Kendall, he had to take the phone away from his ear. Captain had screamed and hollered with a few choice words at the news. "How the hell could this happen!?"

Captain Kendall gave Detectives Armano and Snyder their orders and added, "Keep your eyes and ears open. Don't take chances. This guy is crazy and dangerous, the likes of which we have never seen before. Call if you need help. I will have several men scouring the woods around the hospital. Stay put for now until I tell you otherwise."

Armano had stayed mute until his captain quieted down and answered, "Yes Sir!" Armano found his hand was shaking as he ended the call. He looked at Snyder and sighed. She patted him on the arm and nodded.

They stood in front of Dan as he looked at them in surprise to see them back so soon.

Dan observed the detectives whose faces were white. They were definitely in shock over something. He waited to hear what it was.

"Dan, do you know where Dr. Roberts went with his family? You need to call them and tell them to come back here right away. They could be in danger if Sage returns. We don't know where he is right now. Per our Captain, everyone is to stay put for the time being."

"I know where they are. They're at The Windy Port Restaurant. Okay, Detective Armano, but what happened?"

Detective Armano relayed what they had seen out in the parking lot, two dead bodies of the FBI agents, and no sign of Sage.

Dan quickly called Dr. Darien Roberts or Dr. Robert Fontana as he now knew him and reported what the detectives had told him. Dan settled back in his seat and watched the activity outside in the parking lot. There were more policemen and FBI agents out there than he had ever seen on TV.

Dan was worried about the good doctor and his family. What if this maniac returned? Dan called

Sharynn, Dr. Fontana's secretary, to let her know what was happening.

"Are you kidding me, Dan? What are the police doing about it?" Sharynn's anger got the better of her. She couldn't forget the time this man tried to kidnap her to do who knows what to her. Luckily she used her head and a siren and pepper spray to save herself from him.

"Don't worry yourself over it, Sharynn. I am here to keep an eye on things and the two detectives are on alert also. They are down here in the lobby and not going anywhere. If you need me, please call. Okay?"

"Thanks. Um, Dan, do you think you would like to go out for a drink sometime?" Sharynn tapped her fingernails on her computer as she held her breath waiting for an answer. She had become drained from waiting for Dan to ask her out.

"Oh, um, sure, I would love to. I've been meaning to ask you that question myself. I was too nervous that you would say 'no.' I'll stop up there and walk you to your car tonight and we can talk some more. Okay?"

"Okay, Dan. Thanks. Oh, by the way, did you call Dr. Roberts er, I mean, Dr. Fontana, about all this?"

"Yes, yes, I did. I called him right away as soon as I heard about it from the detectives. The detectives came running back in so fast as if they had seen a ghost. Their faces were white and their hands were actually shaking as they talked to their supervisor."

"Poor Robert and his family. They must be extremely upset and out of their minds. Who knows what this man will do next? Well, I better get finished with some paperwork before the doctor comes back. I know he will want to be busy to keep his mind off this craziness. Talk to you later, Dan. Bye."

"Bye, Sharynn." Dan hung up the phone and gazed off into the distance as he imagined going out with this gorgeous woman he had loved too long from afar.

***

Detective Armano paced the floor while he spoke on the phone to his Captain once again. "Yes Sir, I understand. We'll report anything out of the ordinary. Yes, I see the FBI agents are out there and more police from surrounding communities are searching the woods. I can't believe it either. Okay, will do. Sir."

"What did he say now, Armano?" Detective Snyder waited for an answer. She had tried to figure out what was going on but was still in shock.

"Well, you know how Cap is. He wants us to stay inside and keep an eye out for the Doc and his family, and report anything. They are heading back here. Cap wants this guy and he will do whatever it takes to get him with or without the FBI's help."

"Wow, this is insane, Chris! How the hell did he get out of the cuffs and attack two armed agents like that? He's more dangerous than I imagined. We better watch our backs too. If he could do that to them, what would he do to us? I am no karate expert but can handle myself quite well. What about you, Armano?"

"Huh, oh, yeah I can take care of myself, Snyder. I've seen some of your karate moves, by the way. They are nothing like in the movies by Jackie Chan or Jet Li," Armano chuckled as he bent over holding his stomach.

"Funny man, you are, Armano!" Snyder elbowed him as she walked by.

"Hey, watch out there. You are hitting a police officer!" Armano warned still snickering.

"Listen Armano, we should have checked Sage over carefully. We might have found that pin he had to get out of the cuffs. The FBI agents didn't check him over either."

"Yeah, that's why they lost their lives. Cap didn't say anything about that other than the FBI Director was incensed over the ineptitude of his agents to miss that."

"Oh boy, Armano. We had better watch our backs and everybody else's. We won't make the same mistake as they did."

"For sure! Snyder, you take the back entrance and keep watch. I'll stay here and watch the front. We need to be ready in case he tries to sneak in again. I'll have Dan check with the other staff to be on alert too. The alarms are on, so don't try to open any doors unless you let Dan know ahead of time. He has the camera views on all doors and hallways and will let us know if he spots him."

"Great! If Dan spots him it's already too late, Armano. You know that, don't you?" Snyder cringed thinking of what the man had already done to several women and now the two agents. She had never had a suspect as dangerous or scary as this one. Snyder hoped she would never see another one like him.

"Um, yeah, don't worry, Snyder, we can take care of him." Armano doubted whether they could but he would never let his partner know his insecurities. He was frightened as hell but would never admit it.

***

Captain Kendall was on the phone with the FBI Director once again. The Director was more irate than the last time. Well, after all, his men didn't do their job right. Captain would be upset if his men had been that careless not to have checked the perpetrator for a pin. That was a shame to have lost two good men that way. Now Captain wanted his men to be on alert even more so. He wanted to be the one to catch this son of a bitch.

Captain Kendall was a fearless man but today he wasn't feeling as self-assured having a dangerous perp on the loose. This man was more than unpredictable, he was insane, and no sane man could imagine what an unstable man's next move would be. He would have to think outside the box. Even if the FBI was on the case he wouldn't rest until this man was put away for good. His main job now was to take care of his men and watch over Robert Fontana and his family. They were the ones in the most danger.

Let the FBI do what they have to do. He would keep his eyes and ears open and be vigilant. He had to be ready for anything.

**

Sharynn busied herself with her files and paperwork on each patient, organizing everything for Dr. Fontana. She kept looking over her shoulder in case…well, just in case.

She heard footsteps outside her office door and turned to see Dr. Harper returning from his rounds. Dr. Harper was taking care of the patients until Dr. Fontana returned.

"Hi Sharynn. What's wrong?" Dr. Harper came around her desk to put his hands on her trembling shoulders. In fact, Sharynn was shaky all over. Her eyes misted over and she hung her head.

"Oh, Dr. Harper, something terrible has happened," Sharynn continued to explain all the shocking details of Sage's escape.

"What? You've got to be kidding! How did he get away? Does all the staff know?"

"Dan is probably informing all the staff now as we speak. He told me and I thought I should let you know as soon as I saw you."

"I appreciate that, Sharynn. What are the police doing now?"

"The two detectives that were here before came right back after they found the FBI agents' bodies. They planned to stay here to protect us. We can't leave until they give us the okay. It looks like we may have dinner here tonight. That's not so bad but we may have to make it ourselves since the staff will probably be going home soon after feeding the patients. Dr. Fontana and his family are on their way back here. They will be staying here too for now." Sharynn commenced her anxious rambling.

"That's okay. I'll have to call my wife and let her know I may be late getting home." Dr. Harper looked at his phone that was vibrating and saw a text from Dan.

"Looks like Dan sent me the same info on a text. He must have tried to reach me earlier but I had silenced my phone while visiting with patients.

Excuse me Sharynn, I need to call my wife. I will be in my office. Please let me know when Dr. Fontana returns."

"Sure, Dr. Harper, give my best to your wife. You may not want to tell her why you are staying later. She'll be upset and worried about you."

"Yeah, my thinking exactly, Sharynn. I'll come up with something for now. But she will find out soon enough from the news."

"Oh, that's right. It's probably all over the news."

Sharynn turned on the TV that was in the corner of her office and watched what was happening outside the hospital. Cold tremors ran up and down her body as she observed the FBI agents' bodies being placed inside the ambulance or most likely coroner's van.

Footsteps could be heard again coming down the hall. Sharynn armed herself with an umbrella in one hand and her pepper spray in the other, ready for anything.

CHAPTER FIVE

Sage dragged the body of the camp manager outside the cabin. He looked for signs of anyone around. It was deathly quiet and dark. Just the way he liked it. Darkness always covered things over but once the light returned he had to make sure all evidence of the manager's body was disposed.

Sage almost didn't hear the man coming into the cabin. The man had crept in quietly trying to surprise the invader of his cabin. Sage had been in the bathroom rummaging around for towels and sheets when he heard the creaking of the floor boards. He flipped off the lights and grabbed a plunger and hit the man in the face giving him enough time to push the man down and deliver a fatal blow to his head with the heel of his hand. The man wore a uniform with his name and Camp Tambor Manager on his shirt.

Sage always felt relief and deep satisfaction after a kill. Especially, he surmised, when it was a close call and his own life was in the balance.

He looked down at the shocked expression on the face of the dead man as Sage dragged his body out to the woods looking for a place to dig another grave. The body count was building. It wasn't as enjoyable as when he had more time to plan a kill. But he knew there would be more bodies and more time to plan how to kill them.

What Sage didn't know was there were more visitors coming this weekend - two families with children, an older couple and a group of teenagers.

He grabbed a flashlight off the wall in the kitchen before going outside to dig a grave for the manager. He put it on the ground next to where he planned to dig.

Sage patted down the dirt after his last shovelful, wiped the sweat off his brow with the borrowed t-shirt, and sighed. This is not how he had planned to begin his adventure – digging graves! He usually deposited his kills out in the open to get attention and some notoriety. The bodies of the old woman, her dog, and this man might never be found. But he was keeping track of his kills anyway. Today was a busy day – three kills.

He turned off the flashlight and went back into the cabin, showered and put on the clean clothes he had pilfered from the old lady's house. The few clothes he had taken would suffice for now until he could buy more unless he had to dig more graves, he chuckled.

He began making up the bed with the sheets he had found and would call it a night. He was worn-out from all the heavy digging. He wanted to be rested in case he had any other unwanted visitors in the morning.

Early the following day light was filtering through the slats of the blinds in Sage's cabin bedroom. He stretched and climbed out of bed, dropped down to do his 100 pushups and stretches, and karate katas to begin his day. He always felt better after a workout. It kept him fresh and limber.

He went into the kitchen to see what he could scrounge up for a decent breakfast. He wanted more than a can of beans. He found a box of waffles tucked in the back of the freezer covered in a thick layer of ice. The waffles looked pathetic but upon opening the box the waffles appeared to still be edible. He popped four small waffles into the four slice toaster on the counter and searched around for some syrup or sugar to top it off.

He found a bottle of honey in the cabinet and drizzled a good amount to cover up the freezer burned taste. The waffles would do until he could go shopping in the little town on the other side of the lake.

Sage was cleaning up when he heard the crunching of gravel and the sound of cars coming up the drive to the manager's office. He looked out and noticed two families with kids, an older couple, and several teenagers entering the office.

He made a snap decision and walked out of the cabin and headed for the office. This would make a perfect cover for him. No one would think to look for him working out in the open. He had shaved his head due to thinning hair, but hadn't bothered to shave his face, liking the feel of his whiskers which would grow fast and provide him with a new persona.

He opened the door to the office and called out to the group of people who were sitting, standing, and waiting around for someone to check them in. Sage put on his best smile. "Welcome to Camp Tambor. My name is Brad. Are you all together?"

An older gentleman stepped forward. "No, I am Jeremiah and this is my wife, Gayle. We booked one of your cabins for the weekend. We were told to come at this time to check in."

Others stepped forward and announced that they were told the same thing to check in early. Each group introduced themselves as they waited behind Jeremiah and Gayle to be checked in. Sage opened up the book and noted each name and checked them off as he pulled keys out of cubby holes to match the number of the cabin that they each had been assigned. Lucky for him the manager was quite organized and had done all the work ahead of time.

He had noted the placement of the cabins and numbers when he had perused the area for the farthest secluded cabin, number twelve, for himself. This enabled him to be able to direct the visitors to the correct cabins while he carried their luggage.

He took the elderly couple to their cabin first which was the one closest to the office, number one. The next group was the family with three children assigned to cabin, number two. The other family that had two children and a dog went to cabin, number four, and the group of six teenagers, half boys and the other half girls were sent to a larger cabin, number ten. They were all quite a distance apart from him giving everyone some privacy which Sage appreciated. He didn't particularly want any company. He knew that once the guests were situated they would be out and about and nosing around.

Sage went back to the office building and looked around for whatever he could make use of. He picked up a Swiss Army knife, flashlight, and matches, pocketed what money was in the cash register, fifty bucks, and hoisted a folded tent, blanket, sleeping bag off the shelf along with a canteen, prepackaged food, some beef jerky, and finally he grabbed a gun that was behind the door of the inner office. He needed to get out of there quickly. The manager had a car parked in the back of the office. Hopefully he had left his keys in the car or somewhere in the office. He searched around but couldn't find them, then moved to the car. Luckily for him, Sage found an extra set under the carpet on the driver's side. Most likely the main set was in the manager's pocket which was now under three feet of dirt. He wasn't about to dig him up. If he hadn't found this set of keys he would have had to steal one of the guests' cars then ditch it and find another later.

After stashing all the supplies from the office into the manager's car, Sage jogged back to his cabin. He packed his things and locked up the cabin after he noticed a master key on the chain in his hand. He jogged back to the office and got into the manager's car, a Jeep in pretty good condition. As he backed his way out of the lake area he almost ran over a guest and his dog walking up the path from the lake.

The guest waved at him as he passed and Sage smiled and returned the greeting as he pulled onto the dirt road and burned rubber leaving the area. He checked the gas gauge and noted more than half a tank. Sage sighed and drove on looking for any signs of other lake cottages in the area where he could hide out for the next night. He hoped no one would go looking for the manager or his car yet.

There were several lakes around the area and he would hop from one to another until he could find the perfect hiding spot. He planned to sleep outside if need be now that he had a sleeping bag and a tent.

Sage drove on for over an hour but had to stop for a break and something to eat. He spied a small store with a restaurant attached and a gas station. He filled up at the pump, pocketed the keys after locking up the Jeep, and went into the restaurant.

A waitress moseyed over to his table with a dirty menu in her hand as she snapped her gum and looked him over. She was well over the hill with breasts that hung low and ankles that welled over her grubby shoes. She winked at him and asked in a sing song voice, "What can I get for ya?"

Sage was not in the mood to be toyed with and grunted, "Give me a minute with the menu, will ya?"

"Oh, sure, honey. No problem, take your time. That is all I have, time." She turned and went back to the kitchen to talk to the cook. The cook shook his head as he looked Sage's way. The waitress pulled down a plastic cup and filled it with ice and water and headed back to Sage's table with a smile.

"Here's some cold water to wet your whistle, young man. Are you from these parts? You certainly look fit and strong. You must be a weight lifter, huh?" Saggy boobs ogled Sage some more as she leaned forward to give him a better view of her breasts which were now hanging closer to his face.

Sage kept the dirty menu between him and the woman's chest and ignored her flirtatious remarks and loose boobs. He slammed down the menu and turned his attention back to the startled waitress who cowered away from him. She adjusted her bra and tapped her broken nails on her pad of paper as she tried not to look at Sage's glowering eyes.

"I can come back in a few if you need more time to make a decision, sir."

"No, I'll have a cheeseburger, fries and a chocolate shake and make it snappy!"

"Oh, yes sir, right away." Swollen ankles hurried back to the kitchen to put in his order.

Sage looked over at the cook and waitress as they had their heads together whispering about him. He chuckled as he saw the shock on her face and now the nervous expression on the cook as he threw a burger and some fries onto the grill.

Sage needn't worry about being bothered by Saggy Boobs anymore. He couldn't keep the stupid grin off his face. Sage was having a good time keeping the cook and waitress on edge. The cook turned up the heat to cook the burger faster. The waitress held out the plate, with ketchup ready, to pick up the food.

Saggy came back in short order with his lunch and placed it in front of him as she backed away saying, "Will there be anything else, sir?"

"No, that's all. Now leave me alone to enjoy it. I can't stand the sight of you another minute," Sage laughed out loud and strong as he took his first bite.

He was surprised how good it was! It didn't need any ketchup, and the fries were thin and crispy. Excellent lunch! He hadn't realized how hungry he had become. He finished his lunch within fifteen minutes and threw a twenty down on the table to cover his eight dollar lunch and left. The waitress rushed over to pick up the money and waved it in the air at the cook whose eyes opened wide and smiled.

Sage didn't know if they were happy to receive such a big tip or that they were relieved to see him leave. He didn't care one way or the other. He had a full belly and was happy having given them both a fright. He might come back there another time to say, 'hello,' Sage guffawed as he drove away from the greasy diner.

Sage wanted to put some more distance between him and Tambor Lake. He figured the guests would be looking for him soon. *They might call the police to report me missing. Ha, that would be funny! Now I am not only a murderer at large but a missing cabin manager. I wear many hats*, he thought, with a chuckle.

Sage stopped at the next gas station he saw and filled up once again. He grabbed a few snacks and water bottles. He continued on but slowed down, after driving for three more hours, when he saw another lake with plenty of woods in which to hide. Perfect! He would need some time to set up his tent and look around the area to make sure he would be secure and not be seen from the road.

He had everything set up, tucked far enough into the woods. Now he would have to hunt for dinner. He planned to build a fire behind some large rocks that would provide some cover. He set a trap that he had found inside the trunk of the Jeep and hunkered down.

A cute little bunny came hopping along and sniffed his way close to the trap. Sage waited.

CHAPTER SIX

Dr. Fontana, under the watchful eyes of the police escort, opened the door of the limo and assisted his mother, sister, and her husband out of the back seat followed by Mariah and her boyfriend, Tony. Robert had called ahead to Dan to alert him about their return in a few minutes.

Robert had spoken with Captain Kendall about the safety of his family. Captain Kendall had assured Robert that his men were not going anywhere until Sage was caught. Captain inquired whether Robert had some place for them to bunk down for a couple of days until they knew Sage's whereabouts.

Robert agreed about that and appreciated their protection. "I have some extra rooms that are not being used by patients on the first floor. I will set them up there and take care of their food too. I have an excellent chef and kitchen staff. Your men might like the food so much they may not want to leave." Robert tried to lighten things up but felt his nerves getting the better of him.

"That's kind of you, Dr. Fontana, but my budget will take care of room and board. You will be reimbursed for your troubles. I appreciate that you can accommodate my detectives though. Your family will need to stay put for the same amount of time."

"Yes, I understand, Captain. I have rooms for them too. We will be fine. Please let me know when you have more information about Sage. I want him caught."

"Oh, I will call as soon as I know more. Don't worry, Dr. Fontana, I plan to put him away this time once and for all with or without the help of the FBI."

"Thank you, Captain. I appreciate that. Well, I have to get my family settled now. Talk to you soon, I hope."

"Yes, so do I. Take care, Doctor."

***

Dan opened the doors to the hospital for Dr. Fontana and his family. He reiterated what the detectives had told him.

Detective Armano stepped forward and shook hands with Dr. Fontana. "My partner, Detective Snyder, is keeping watch over the rear of the building and I will be situated at the front. We will be here until Captain Kendall tells us otherwise. I would suggest that you all get settled in your rooms. Don't worry about anything. We have a job to do."

"Thank you, Detective Armano. We appreciate all that you are doing. I spoke with your captain and told him that I can provide rooms and meals for you and your partner."

"That's kind of you, Doctor."

"Dan, can you please show the detectives to rooms 1 and 2? I will have Miguel get dinners for you and the detectives. If you need a break, please call Sharynn and one of us will come down to relieve you. It may be a long night for us until we know where Sage is."

"No problem, Doc." Turning to Detective Armano, Dan directed him to the rooms.

Detective Armano called his partner, Snyder, on his phone to let her know where they would be staying for the night. They would have to take turns guarding the entrances in shifts.

"No problem, Snyder. Heard food is top notch here. It may not be such a bad place to be on lookout."

"You would think of food first, Armano!" Snyder scoffed.

"Well, a man's got to eat!" Armano chuckled as he looked over the room and used the restroom before going back to his station at the front door.

***

Robert entered his office and was nearly hit in the head by a swinging umbrella.

"What in the world are you doing, Sharynn?"

Sharynn stood with her umbrella and pepper spray, finger on nozzle, prepared to protect herself.

"I'm so sorry, Dr. Fontana. I didn't realize it was you. I've been a little jumpy since this happen."

Robert's family stepped into his office and laughed at the sight of Sharynn with an umbrella and pepper spray pointed at Robert.

"What's going on?" Beatrice asked as she tried to keep her smile at bay over the look of shock on her son's face.

"Nothing, Mother, everything is fine. Sharynn is being a little too cautious. Aren't you, Sharynn?"

Robert smiled, trying to lighten things up a little. He knew why Sharynn was anxious. She had every right to be.

"I really am sorry, Dr. Fontana. I…well, I guess I was being cautious." Sharynn hung her head and put down her weapons as she headed over to the coffee and prepared another pot. "Anyone want a cup of coffee?"

"Sure, a coffee would be great about now. It's okay, Sharynn. Please relax. We have extra rooms available for all of you. I'll get the housekeeping staff on duty to get the rooms ready for you. Miguel will be preparing dinner for everyone. We can eat in the dining room. We can talk more then."

Robert called the nurses on duty, Cara and Laura, and instructed them to prepare the patients for dinner.

"Certainly, right away. We heard about Sage. So sorry to hear that he got away. Laura and I will take turns caring for the patients and schedule our meals and rest periods."

"Thank you, Cara. That would be helpful. I appreciate everything that you are doing. I promise to give you both time off after this is over."

"Oh, thank you, but we want to do our part. We can handle things." Cara contained her enthusiasm as she silently did a happy dance over the thought of time off.

His next call was to housekeeping to alert them to prepare the empty rooms for the detectives and his family.

"Okay, Dr. Fontana. I'll let you know when the rooms are ready," Matilda, Head of Housekeeping replied.

"Appreciate that, thanks." Robert ended the call and related to his family that the rooms should be ready soon for them. In the meantime, they could freshen up in the bathroom in his office.

***

Miguel had gone immediately to the kitchen to let his staff know that they would not be going home yet and were needed to prepare dinner not only for the patients but also for the hospital staff, the detectives, and Dr. Fontana and his family.

Miguel, discussed with his staff, what he wanted them to prepare and to order any supplies that were needed to get through the evening into the next day.

He told his staff to call home to alert their families they wouldn't be going home tonight.

"Let's take one day at a time. If we don't get home by tomorrow night you can call and update them on what is happening."

"Okay, Miguel. Thanks. I'll send Ricardo up to the rooms with the patients' trays first then I will take the meals to the dining room for our guests."

"That's fine, Manuel. Don't forget to put aside dinners for yourself and Ricardo. Doc has prepared rooms for everyone."

"Thanks, Miguel. But that's not necessary. We can crash on the couches in the lounge tonight. If that's okay with you."

"Okay, but as long as you are sure."

"I'm used to sleeping on couches. My wife is famous for relegating me to the couch when she's angry with me."

"Is that okay with you, Ricardo?" Miguel inquired.

"Huh, oh yeah, that's fine. My wife will probably be happy I'm not going to be home. Then, she won't have to cook my dinner. She hates to cook!"

Manuel laughed and bumped fists with Ricardo as they went about preparing the dinners. Miguel watched their easy camaraderie and felt fortunate to have such good men on his staff that he could depend on.

***

Four police officers and two FBI agents were still moving through the woods surrounding the hospital. They noticed some bent branches as they got to the end of the woods. They examined, on closer inspection, the dirt and snow that was flattened down by footprints.

The FBI agents looked around the area and spied the houses that were within walking distance from where they now stood. They knew what their next step would be.

The FBI agents called in to report that they would be canvassing the neighborhood.

CHAPTER SEVEN

Back at Tambor Lake the visitors were sitting inside the office and calling out to the manager. They had settled their stuff in their individual cabins and were looking for something to eat for lunch. They had banded together as a group now since they had arrived once they could not find him.

Their cabins were devoid of food supplies. The manager had told them when they booked the cabin that there would be food supplies included in the price for breakfast and lunch inside their cabin. They needed to pick up some supplies if the manager did not come back.

The six teenagers offered to go out looking in the woods surrounding the lake. "Maybe the manager has gone fishing or trapping. We are all able to walk for miles. He has to be here somewhere."

When no one responded the teens set off on their own. It was better than standing around with old people who didn't know what they were doing.

The man with the dog who had seen the manager leaving the area spoke up, "I saw him leaving three hours or so ago. He peeled rubber leaving. He kicked up plenty of dust and pebbles that frightened my dog."

"I wonder what could have made him leave so suddenly," Jeremiah queried as he looked at his wife who was wearing a rejected expression. She had planned to take a ride in a boat.

"Well, there isn't much we can do about the supplies until he comes back," one father stated, trying to cheer up his three children who were getting antsy.

Another announced, "It's too chilly to go swimming but we could find where the manager keeps the keys to the boats. There is one big enough for a family of ten. Anybody want to join us in searching for the keys?"

"Sure, why not," another father suggested. "Let's start here in the office and behind the counter."

While one family searched the office thoroughly, the other family went out to the boat house. It was soon evident that the keys were not in the office. Most likely the keys were kept in the boat house.

The family with two kids and the dog joined the other family in the boat house to help them search. It was better than sitting around waiting for the manager to come back. The man walking his dog, who had seen the manager leave in a hurry, suspected that he wasn't coming back any time soon anyway.

Jeremiah and his wife, Gayle, sat in the comfy chairs in the office and waited. They were not going to exhaust themselves. The others were a lot younger and more able to search than they were.

Gayle noticed a coffee pot, cups, creamers and sugars in the corner of the room. Sadly, she noticed it was empty. She got up slowly, rubbed her aching back, and went to find water and coffee to make a pot.

"I'll be right back, Jerry. I think I know where to look for water and coffee."

Gayle went behind the counter and opened the door to the manager's office. There was a storage area well stocked with supplies of food, coffee, paper products, and a refrigerator with milk and drinks. She also noticed some enticing packages of biscotti on the shelves. She pulled down two packages of chocolate ones and set them aside as she filled the coffee pot with water from the sink nearby and prepared the pot. With cookies in one hand and the pot in the other she went back to the front room and plugged in the pot. Soon the aroma of coffee surrounded them.

Such a pleasant and calming smell, Jerry thought, as he watched Gayle open up a package of cookies and offer one to him. He felt a deep love for his wife of nearly forty years. She didn't have much time left before she lost more of herself. This damn disease, Alzheimer's, was slowly taking her away from him.

She had always taken care of him. Now it was his time to take care of her, hence this trip to the lake. She had always wanted to take a ride on a boat and look at the beautiful scenery. The leaves were changing and soon it would be too cold to venture out.

The families returned from the boat house with keys in hand, enough for two boats which would hold a dozen people. When they smelled the fresh coffee and the kids saw the cookies, they put their boat ride on hold a little longer.

Gayle spoke up, much to Jeremiah's surprise, "There's plenty of food in the back room if anyone is still hungry. I only brought out the cookies but there's more of them and other stuff too." She smiled and nodded at Jeremiah and sat quietly looking down at her hands.

"Thanks, Ma'am, that's good to know," one of the father's said as he watched his kids gobbling up the cookies. One mother went to find milk for the children.

Once the cookies, milk, and coffee were gone the families each took a boat and offered Jeremiah and Gayle a hand to come on board whichever one they chose. Gayle loved dogs so she went with the family that had a dog.

The teens were walking around the lake and noticed the boats heading out from the dock. They ran back and yelled out to the boaters, "Hey, can we come too?"

One family yelled back, "Sorry, no room for all of you. Go to the boat house and get one for yourselves. The keys are on the wall next to the boats and numbered. Have fun!"

The teens ran ahead and were at the boat house in short order. There was only one boat left besides a couple of canoes which were too small for all six of them. They grabbed the keys off the hook and jumped into the boat. They argued over who would drive. "Oh, come one Reg, let me drive first," Steve begged.

"Okay, but I will be next, then Chace can take over."

"Hey, what about us?" The girls whined in unison.

"Don't get so impatient, ladies! You will all get your turn. Let's go once around the lake then we can take turns after that."

"Oh, all right," the girls reluctantly agreed.

The air was cool and brisk once they got underway. But everyone was bundled up. The teens were having a wonderful time until their boat ran out of gas. They waved down the other boats and yelled, "We need a tow. We ran out of gas!"

The two boats drifted over to the teens and using a rope they tied it to one of their boats and slowly towed the teens' boat back to the dock.

Faces were rosy and glowing from their excursion which had been well over two hours long. They tied the boats up at the dock and headed back to their respective cabins after thanks were shared around.

The teens were starving as always and looked around the cabin for anything they could eat. The manager had told them that there would be some basic supplies such as bread, coffee and some canned and boxed goods. They would be included in the price of the cabin. Evidently he had forgot to stock their cabin. This cabin was empty of any supplies except towels and paper goods. They jumped into their two cars with the hope of finding a restaurant close by. They did not hear about the well-stocked manager's office.

It was too late for lunch but still early for dinner. They couldn't wait any longer to eat. They soon came to a restaurant and a store attached with a gas station in front. While the boys filled the gas tank at the pump, the girls visited the restrooms then went into the restaurant to find a table.

The same waitress was there that had earlier waited on Sage. She was still snapping her gum as she exchanged greetings with the three girls and set down menus.

"Are you expecting those fellas outside to join you?"

"Yes, they'll be right in."

"Take your time. I'll bring some waters in the meantime. Do you want to hear the specials?"

"Um, yeah, I guess. Hey, Nat and Ang, do you want to hear the specials?" Stacy giggled as she rolled her eyes at the waitress and her droopy boobs, swollen ankles and snapping gum.

Droopy boobs didn't wait for an answer and droned on about the specials, meatloaf, chili, and chicken noodle soup.

The boys came in and plopped themselves down and nearly chocked with laughter when they got a gander of the waitress and her boobs which almost reached her knees when she bent over to place their waters on the table.

The girls poked the boys in the ribs and giggled. The girls finally got themselves under control when the waitress cleared her throat to ask, "Well, what would you like?"

The boys ordered burgers, fries and chocolate shakes along with the girls. The waitress looked up from her pad and announced, "I guess this is the day for burgers, fries and shakes. The strange guy that came in here earlier ordered the same thing. He was a mite scary though. Watch out for him. He had a shaved head with some whiskers on his chin and scary brown eyes that looked right through ya. I shiver to think of them. He headed north. I would give him a wide birth if you are heading that way."

The girls put their heads together and whispered. "That sounds like the manager of Tambor Lake, doesn't it? Yeah, I thought he was a little creepy the way he looked at us. I'm glad he headed north. Maybe he won't be back."

The boys nodded in agreement. "If he doesn't come back we can go to another lake. We can get some supplies at the store next door before we head back."

"Yeah, that's a good idea, guys. We could pick up some frozen pizzas, snacks, and stuff to make s'mores later tonight by the camp fire and cocoa with small marshmallows too," Stacy announced.

"Ooh, that sounds yummy! Now I'm really starving. I hope the burgers are good here!" Nat stressed.

When the food arrived the teens attacked it and all talking ceased as they munched happily on the delicious burgers, fries and shakes.

"Wow, these are the best burgers I've ever had!" Reg announced in between large bites which he nearly choked on while trying to talk.

"Yeah, I agree, yum!" Steven mumbled as he stuffed more fries into is already full mouth.

"Well, at least we won't starve while we're here at the lake. We can come here again during the week for more burgers," Chace muttered as he slurped on his shake.

"Sounds good to us too," the girls chimed in.

After stocking up on the supplies for s'mores and other goodies, since they knew they would be hungry in a few hours again, the teens decided to drive around and see some of the sights and check out the other lakes. A few hours later they headed back to the lake cabin.

When they arrived they kept their eyes out for the creepy manager in case he came back. After listening to the waitress and watching the frightened expression on her sallow face they were anxious about seeing him again.

Being adventuresome the boys roamed around their cabin and walked over to the cabin that the manager had come out of, number twelve. They were curious about what he might have in there. Maybe they could find some interesting stuff to share with the girls.

They tried the door but it was locked. They walked around the sides and back checking all windows until they came to the back door. It was unlocked.

Opening it slowly they peered inside. Reg pulled out his cell, put on the flashlight and looked around with Steve and Chace right behind him.

The place looked lived in but there was nothing out of the ordinary there. The boys rummaged around the kitchen and bedroom and bath for anything they could use for their own cabin. They snatched some toilet paper and extra towels and turned to leave.

"Wait one minute, guys. I saw something on the floor that was shiny. Look at this! It's a woman's ring."

"Let me see that, Chace! Wow, looks like it could be a wedding ring with small diamonds. I've seen one like that before. It's called a waterfall ring. My grandmother has one. It's not worth too much but it could buy us a few dinners maybe."

"I'll keep it safe," Chace stated as he swiftly pocketed it before the others could object.

Walking back outside to the driveway they noticed the car. "Hey get a load of this old car! My grandfather had one similar to this. He always said he loved the cars back then better than the cars of today. Maybe we can try to start it and take it for a ride," Steven said.

"Na, I don't think so. What if the manager comes back and finds it missing. I don't think I want to deal with him," Reg said.

The boys agreed and went back the way they came.

The girls were out in front of the cabin when the boys returned trying to start a fire in the pit for the s'mores and to keep warm. They had heated up the pizzas and set them by the pit to keep warm. They held steaming mugs of cocoa as they picked up small sticks and threw them into the pit. The weather was getting chillier and they wanted to stay outside until about 10:00 pm but didn't want to freeze to death.

The boys roamed around looking for more brush to add to the pit and walked behind cabin twelve again.

"Hey guys, look at this," Chace said as he noticed a smooth area under a tree as they all began to pick up some branches.

"Looks like someone was digging here. Whoever did this was in a hurry. They left the shovel lying next to the tree," Steven announced.

"What are you going to do, Chace? No, we are not going to dig up whatever is in there! That is too creepy for words!" Reg's voice shook.

"Maybe it's buried treasure. He didn't like the idea of digging either.

"Steve, come on and help me. Reg is afraid of ghosts and goblins in the night," Chace coaxed.

"Ah come on, guys, this is not right. You have no idea what you are going to find," Reg begged.

"Oh, go back and help the girls with the camp fire, Reg. Let us men take care of this," his friends mocked as they took turns digging.

Reg turned away from them, happy to be far from whatever they would find. He busied himself tending to the fire which was now providing the area with some warmth as the girls sipped their hot cocoa.

Screams suddenly broke the silence as Chace and Steve came running back to the camp fire.

As they ran they pulled out their cells to call the police.

CHAPTER EIGHT

Robert escorted his family to their rooms once they were ready and made sure everyone was comfortable. He met with Miguel to see how food preparations were coming along. He knew he could trust Miguel to handle every detail but he found that he needed to keep busy to calm his nerves.

The dining room, which was seldom used, since the patients preferred to eat in their rooms, was set and decorated for fall. Miguel had carved a pumpkin and set it in the middle of the extensive table with a large candle giving the room an eerie glow.

Robert flipped on some more lights to erase the shadows in the corners. He knew he was letting Sage get to him but he couldn't help being cautious. It wasn't only his life on the line now but all of his family's lives too.

Miguel watched from the doorway as Robert flipped on the lights. "Doc, are you okay?"

"Oh, hi Miguel. Thanks for setting the table and decorating it. It will put my family at ease. I'm …yes, I'm okay. A little anxious until Sage is found."

"You don't have to explain, Robert. I understand. I saw him in action and know how dangerous he can be. I plan on staying close to help in any way I can."

"Thanks, Miguel. You do enough already. Thank your kitchen staff for me too. They are tireless to keep working like this. I plan to reward all of you for the extra work you have put in. So what gastronomical delight did you create for tonight's dinner?"

"Well, I don't know if it's a gastronomical delight but it will be tasty. My staff is preparing a special chicken recipe as we speak. It should be ready within an hour or less. We will be feeding the patients first and then everyone else. Is that okay? Hey, Robert, I thought you and your family went out to dinner."

"Ah, yes but we got Dan's message about Sage and had to come right back without dinner. But I think your food is probably better anyway."

"Thanks. Nice of you to say."

"That's perfect, Miguel! We always keep our patients happy first, then we can relax and enjoy dinner together. I'll go see my family and let them know when to come down. See you in an hour."

Robert went to check on things in the lobby. He would feel more secure if he could see that all was well for himself. Dan was sitting at his station, eyes on all cameras.

"How's things, Dan?"

"Oh, hi Doc. All's quiet for now. The police officers and FBI agents are looking around through the woods. They haven't come back yet. Maybe they found him." Under his breath Dan whispered, *we can only hope.*

"I doubt if they did, Dan. Sage is too clever for his own good. He has probably found a place to hunker down right out in the open. He better watch out though. These police officers and FBI agents are smarter than he realizes. We are fortunate to have two clever detectives watching over us," Robert stated as Detective Armano came alongside him.

"Thank you, Dr. Fontana, for your confidence in us. We'll do our best to keep you safe. Haven't seen any activity outside for a while. They must have found some clues in their search."

The detective's radio crackled to life. Detective Armano listened in and called out to Snyder. "Did you hear that?"

"Yes, Armano, I think they have a lead."

"Wait, it sounds like more than a lead, Snyder!"

Robert ran to his office to call Captain Kendall and at the same time retrieve his gun out of the safe. He would feel more secure with it on him.

Robert waited anxiously until the dispatch put him through to the Captain. He patted his pocket where the gun now lay.

"Dr. Fontana, is everything all right?"

"That's why I'm calling. I heard, on the detectives' radio, about a lead. Did you find him?"

"Listen, Dr. Fontana. I can't share anything with you at this time except that we did not find Sage. I promised I would contact you as soon as we did. Now don't worry about anything. Stay inside until we can assure that you are safe."

"Please, Captain, can't you give me any idea when you will find him?"

"No, sorry, we don't know that yet. But I promise to inform you as soon as we do. I know you all want to get back to your lives. I need to check out some prospects with my men and get back to you about when you can all go back home. It shouldn't be much longer, I surmise."

"I hope you're right, Captain. Let me know what I can do to help. After all, who knows my brother better than I do?"

"Well, you may be right. But he is too dangerous, and I am responsible for your safety. So, no Doctor, sorry."

***

The two FBI agents moved toward the small house with the white picket fence. There was so sign of movement in or around the house.

One agent knocked on the door as the other one walked around the yard for any signs of life. When he came to the large maple tree he noticed the area in front of the tree looked different from the rest of the yard. Leaves and branches were out of place across a grassless area in an attempt to possibly hide something there. The agent pushed the branches aside and kicked the top layer of dirt which was loose. His foot sunk in a few inches.

He jogged back to the front door where his partner was still standing. No one had come to the door.

"Hey Ray, come back here and give me a hand."

"What's up, Derek?"

"Have a look for yourself."

Ray looked at the dirt that was freshly dug and noticed the shovel lying under the tree. "Looks like we have some digging to do. It could just be a dog. Want me to take first shift?"

"Could be, but it could also been something else. Nah, I found it first. I'll start. When I get bushed you can take over." Derek grabbed the shovel and began to dig.

"I'll call the Director. You know how he is. Wants to know every step we make. Guess he doesn't trust us because of the last two. I still can't believe that they didn't check the perp for any weapons. That was a deadly mistake on their part."

"Yeah, you're right there. We won't make the same mistake when we meet up with him," Derek agreed as he puffed in between shovelfuls.

"I don't know about you but I don't look forward to meeting this son of a bitch. We have come in contact with some dangerous and bizarre characters in our many years with the bureau but never one like this guy."

The FBI agents called the Director to report what they had found. Director Connor was antsy and antagonistic as he asked, "What do you mean you think you found a grave? Whose grave is it?"

"We will know soon, sir. It certainly looks like something was buried in a hurry. We are taking turns digging. We will call you immediately if we find anything."

"You make sure you do that, Agent! Make it soon if you know what is good for you!"

"Oh, yes sir, I will!" Ray rolled his eyes as he looked over at Derek.

"Hey Derek, next time you call Director Connor. He nearly perforated my eardrum with his yelling. We better not make any mistakes like the other agents. If we don't lose our lives making a mistake, Director Connor will kill us."

"Yeah, ha, funny man, Ray! Somehow I think we are not going to meet up with this guy. He is long gone. He's too smart to stay around here. Holy shit...look at this!"

Ray leaned over Derek's shoulder and whistled! "Guess it's your turn to call Director Connor."

***

The policemen who were close behind the FBI agents noticed that the agents were digging in the backyard of a house in the distance beyond the wooded area. They called into the precinct to report what they saw. Captain Kendall wanted to know every move that the FBI were making. He planned to be one step ahead of them if at all possible.

"Good work, men! Keep an eye out and hang close to see what they are doing. Call me back as soon as you know more."

"Yes, Captain, will do."

"Let's get a little closer to see what they find."

The policemen moved along the side of the house away from where the agents were digging. They peered around the back of the house and hid in some bushes as they waited for the Agents to stop digging. They listened as the men spoke evidently to the Director by the sounds of all the 'sirs' they heard.

When they heard one agent yell out to the other they knew something was found. They moved in to find out what it was.

CHAPTER NINE

Miguel's meal was a success as everyone groaned and sighed, bellies full to bursting.

"Well, compliments to the chef and his staff for a thoroughly delicious meal. Thank you, Miguel," Robert announced.

"Thank you, Robert. I'm happy to see everyone enjoyed it. My staff will be pleased too. They worked hard to deliver this meal."

Mariah smiled and nodded in agreement. "Miguel always delivers an excellent meal. I should know. I ate enough of them while I was here."

"Yes, you did, Mariah. You did an unbelievable job of finishing everything I put in front of you," Miguel chuckled.

"I guess I did, Miguel. Still need to lose a few pounds since then." Mariah returned his smile and added a wink.

Robert looked down at his phone and scrolled through his messages. There were none from Captain Kendall.

"What's the matter, dear?" Beatrice asked her son with concern evident in her voice.

"Nothing, Mother. I was checking my messages in case I missed one from Captain Kendall. Nothing yet."

"Don't worry, Robert. He will let you know when he catches Sage. Captain seems like an honorable man and intent on putting Sage away for good."

"I agree, Mother, but you know Sage. He is cagey and not easily caught. He slipped away from the FBI agents once and could do it again. I wonder what they found. Detectives Armano and Snyder were discussing a call they got in whispers and I couldn't catch what they were saying."

Miguel interrupted the conversation as he announced dessert was being served. "Who's ready for some of my apple pie a la mode?"

The serious discussion ended abruptly when everyone oohed and aahed as the slices of pie were being served with coffee.

"Oh Miguel! This pie is the best I have ever had!" Betsy gushed as she spooned in another mouthful.

"Wow, it certainly is!" Everyone joined in agreement.

Mariah nodded her approval and smiled at Miguel but was observing the serious expression on her uncle's face as he ignored the piece of pie in front of him and the vanilla ice cream that was melting on the plate.

She left her seat and walked over to him. "Uncle Robert, are you all right?" She patted him on the arm as she waited for his response.

"Oh, Mariah. I didn't see you there. I'm fine, honey. Not to worry about anything. I was hoping we would hear a word by now. I guess I better eat this pie and ice cream before it melts into mush." Robert mechanically spooned some of it into his mouth.

Seeing that everyone was finishing up their dessert and coffee, Miguel called his staff to come and help clear off the table. It was going to be a long night for him and his men before they got to rest. He would do his share to help them and hopefully soon their lives would get back to normal again.

Robert pushed away the rest of the pie that he didn't finish and announced that he was going to retire. "Well, good night everyone. If you need anything at all please call me. I will be in my apartment but I will keep my cell on."

"Thanks, dear. Sleep well, Robert. I'm sure we will hear by the morning about Sage. We can't stay here forever. We will all go back to our lives soon and the authorities will keep looking for him."

"I hope you're right, Mother. But somehow I don't think this nightmare is going to be over for a long time. He is waiting for us to let down our guard and the authorities too. Once we do he will move in again. He won't rest until we are all dead."

"Robert! Don't talk like that! That is not going to happen, do you hear me? He is only one person and the FBI and police are many. They will find him, don't you worry, son. They WILL find him!"

Mariah nodded and watched her uncle's face. He was fearful and believed what he said about Sage. She hated to admit it, but she agreed with him.

"Uncle Robert, please don't worry. You need to rest. We all need to rest and stay strong to face whatever comes our way."

Tony smiled at the woman he loved. "Yes, everyone. Listen to this woman. She has been through more than anyone of us has and she still is strong and resilient. We need to be strong for her too."

Mariah put her arms around Tony and nestled into his neck and whispered, "Thank you, Tony. I love you."

"I love you too," Tony whispered back, kissing her cheek.

Betsy and Frank excused themselves and left the dining room to go to their room. Ronald followed closely behind escorting his employer, Beatrice, to her room. She was getting on in age and he felt a need to assist her.

Sharynn left soon after to relieve Dan at the front desk so he could eat his dinner. The nurses, Cara and Laura, had left earlier to attend to their patients one more time before resting themselves. The rest of the staff hurried out to their rooms to get some sleep for the day ahead.

Mariah and Tony were left behind. They sipped their cold coffee and held hands.

"What do you think about Sage, Tony? Do you think he is hiding out close by?"

"It's hard to tell. But knowing what we do about Sage I don't doubt that he is nearby. He is unstable and needs to be close enough to watch us, the FBI and police. He likes to be one step ahead."

"I think so too. I'm worried about Uncle Robert. He appears to be distressed. I don't want him to carry the burden of keeping us safe by himself. We all need to take an active role in our own safety."

"Yes, we should, honey. I agree. Let's call it a night. It has been a long eventful day for everyone. Tomorrow may bring some news – hopefully good news that Sage has been caught."

"Okay, Tony. Where is your room? Will you walk me to mine?"

"I'm right next to you. I made sure of that. I'm close in case you need me."

"I like that. I don't want to be far from you ever again."

"Good night, Mariah." Tony pulled her into a tight embrace and kissed her softly as he opened her door.

"Good night, Tony." Mariah kissed him back and sighed. "See you in the morning."

"Bright and early, my love." Tony turned toward the next room, waved and let himself in.

***

Dan finished his dinner and relieved Sharynn from duty and sat back in his chair to observe the activity that suddenly was taking place outside in the parking lot once again. Something was going on out there. He watched the detectives inside as they ran back and forth and spoke in whispers on their cells.

He only hoped he could stay awake a little longer until someone could relieve him after they rested. Doc mentioned he would do that. Maybe he should call Dr. Fontana about the activity. He would want to know if anything was happening.

He buzzed over to the doctor's apartment at the back of the hospital and waited, never taking his eyes off of the police running back and forth in the woods. When an ambulance came by he knew he had to tell the doctor right away.

Robert couldn't get to sleep. When he heard his cell ring, he saw Dan's name come up and quickly answered.

"What's wrong, Dan? Do you need me to cover for you for a while so you can get some rest? I can't sleep anyway."

"Well, maybe, but I wanted to tell you that something is happening outside. There are more police officers and FBI agents now than before and they are running back and forth through the woods, and an ambulance drove by."

"I'll be right there, Dan."

Robert raced back to the front desk where Dan was still holding the phone in his hand. He hadn't realized that the doctor had already hung up."

"Oh sorry Doc, for disturbing you, but I thought you would like to know about things."

"No problem. I appreciate you calling me. Thanks, Dan. Why don't you go catch a few winks? Go to the room at the end of the hall on the right. It's all made up for you. I'll take care of things for now."

"Okay, if you are sure, Doc. Thanks. I'll catch a few and then relieve you."

***

Robert stood at the glass doors and watched what was happening in front of him. There was definitely more activity going on. The police raced through the woods and others drove off in a hurry away from the hospital. The ambulance sped by the parking lot and followed the police cars.

He wanted to follow and find out what they were doing and where they were going in such a hurry. If they had found Sage he was sure that Captain Kendall would have called him by now. There had to be something though that could be connected to Sage. Maybe he wasn't as smart as he thought he was and left some clues behind.

Sage had bitten off more than he could chew, Robert thought. Robert didn't realize how close he was in surmising his brother's predicament. Sage would soon be in much deeper than he could ever imagine the next night.

***

Sage had really lucked out when he unpacked the Jeep and found all kinds of camping equipment, a stove, traps, butane lighter, batteries, lamp, radio and hot packs for his hands and feet to keep warm when the temperatures dipped at night. He could stay out here almost indefinitely and live off the land. The police and FBI would never look for him out in the open. They were too stupid to think about the obvious.

It had only been the second night now since Sage had first started camping out at the lake. He set more traps around the outside of his camp marking them with yellow tape in order to see them clearly. He didn't want to trip one and injure himself.

He had trapped countless rabbits and already had several pelts. If he continued to capture more at this rate he would soon have enough for a future nice warm rabbit coat which would come in handy as it was getting colder.

He wanted to have enough to eat to stay off the grid as long as he could. He would smoke the rabbits he caught to keep them edible for more meals. He had some beef jerky and other snacks to keep up his energy level. Some he had taken from the Camp Manager's office, and the rest he bought at the store when he first came there. He had kept them in case he ran out of food. He had enough to last him a few months or more.

He cleaned up his campsite and began his exercise regime of 100 pushups and karate katas. He was unaware of being watched as he pushed himself through this exhausting set.

***

The bear was hungry and needed to get his final meal before he settled down for the long winter ahead. The weather had suddenly changed with dropping temperatures leading him to move more quickly to find something to eat. The bear sniffed the air around him and headed toward the scent of food and, a human.

CHAPTER TEN

The FBI agents who had found the grave stood by the bodies of the old woman and the dog as the medical examiner examined the bodies to determine the time of death while the forensic pathologist took some samples. More would be done during the autopsy. The FBI Director wanted answers now and had everyone hopping to the same hurried tune.

Director Connor wanted things wrapped up tomorrow. He put pressure on all his staff and no one spoke a word but kept their heads down and mouths shut. No excuses were accepted when he doled out more orders and late night hours for everyone.

Director Connor dreaded talking to Captain Kendall again. Captain was still involved with this case until it was determined that it was Sage who killed the woman and a dog. Hours later that night another body was found at Tambor Lake, reported to him by the Somerset Police because of the APB put out on Sage. He had requested all areas to report anything suspicious.

Director wanted to connect both murders but results were not expected for a few days. He would do his best to rush them. He needed to find this psychopath and find him soon. He expected the body count to increase if he didn't.

He dialed Captain Kendall to discuss once again the ongoing case much to his chagrin.

***

The following evening in the woods by the lakes - Sage stopped in mid pushup when he heard the bear's growl. He knew he couldn't outrun him but he would do his best to outsmart him.

He reached behind and pulled out his knife and stood up slowly. The bear watched him and sniffed the air once again. He smelled the man for fear. Fear had a definitive smell to an animal like this. Fear could be the man's demise.

Sage jumped up and waved his hands and stomped his feet and yelled as loud as he could to make the bear think he was more of a threat. Maybe this would deter the bear from coming after him. Sage had read that doing this could save his life. He didn't know if it would work but doing this was better than waiting around for the bear to attack.

The bear watched the man and moved closer. He kept sniffing the air and put his nose to the ground as he came to the now cold campfire. The bear could smell the rabbit that the man had slaughtered earlier and licked the blood as he moved toward the man and his tent.

Sage grew tired from jumping up and down, and the yelling caused him to lose his voice. The bear didn't seem to be bothered by all this noise and kept coming.

Sage knew that it was kill or be killed as he raced toward the bear and attacked with his knife. The bear swiped his right front paw at Sage knocking him down as the bear stood on his hind legs and roared in anger. Sage's arm was sliced and bleeding. He held it tightly to his chest to curtail the flow of blood. He needed to stay alert long enough to strike with his knife.

Sage kept a tight grip on the knife and tried to slide backwards away from the bear as the bear kept approaching. Sage's left arm was wet with his own blood which continued to flow freely. He couldn't hold onto it to stop the blood and silently prayed (one thing he never did in his life) for more time before he passed out.

He needed more space between himself and the bear if he was going to lift the knife high enough to strike a deadly blow as the bear came down on him. Sage had to find a vital part of the bear to keep the bear from mauling him to death.

The bear looked directly into Sage's eyes and kept coming forward. His eyes were cold and heartless. He had only one thing on his mind – kill this man and get his fill.

The bear ate his fill and hurried away. He was sleepy and needed to find a cave for a long winter's rest.

***

Captain Kendall hung up the phone and sighed. Another body was found, this time at Tambor Lake. The Somerset Police Captain kept in touch with Captain Kendall and mentioned the murder to him.

The Somerset Police received a call from some teens at Camp Tambor. They reportedly found a body. It was supposedly the Camp Manager because his shirt had this printed on it. The teens said that they met a man who claimed to be the manager but he had since disappeared. The police posted an APB on a man impersonating the camp manager last seen at the lake.

Forensics were working around the clock between the police stations and the FBI to discover anything that would connect Sage to these latest murders. Captain Kendall felt a tingling on the back of his neck about this body. Somehow Sage was involved with this one too.

Captain was expecting to hear soon from Director Connor. He knew Director Connor was a man possessed since he lost two of his best men in the field to Sage. Captain also felt much the same way. He had told his men to keep close tabs on what was going on at the house where the FBI agents had recently found the grave of an old woman and a dog. Jurisdiction had not been completely decided enabling both the police and the FBI to keep working together until clues were found to create a delineation.

His phone rang again. Captain Kendall took a deep cleansing breath before answering. His secretary announced, "Captain, Director Connor is on line 2. He says it's urgent."

"Okay, put him through, thanks Laney."

"Captain Kendall."

"Captain, I think we may have some information about the woman and the dog we uncovered. She evidently scratched her assailant. We may be able to identify the skin under her nails. If we can connect it to Sage, you are no longer on this case. It will be solely in our ball park."

"I see. What about the other body at the lake? The medical examiner is working on the body as we speak. I had the Somerset Police send it to my precinct since it could not be determined if it was connected to Sage."

"My men are on their way over there to work with your forensic pathologist to hurry up the investigation. We can't waste time going back and forth, Captain. There may be more lives at stake if we wait."

"I understand, Director. But you need to understand. I want this man as much or more than you do. He has been a pain in my side since he came to New York. There is no reason why we can't continue to work together on this. Two heads are better than one. This maniac already outsmarted two experienced men. We can't afford to lose any more good men, either yours or mine."

"Yes, I agree. Let's keep moving along with the evidence until we find something definitive. If Sage has committed these murders then you need to step aside and let me handle the case. I can keep you in the loop from time to time. Remember, we still don't know where he is. He could show up on your doorstep once again. I could use your eyes and ears on things, especially then."

"You could be right about Sage. He is one slippery perp. I have my men on high alert looking for him in a wide radius. I don't think he has gone too far. We will keep searching for him. You will need all the help you can get to capture him."

"Hmm, let me think about that. Well, I need to check with forensics for more info. I will keep in touch."

Captain Kendall dropped the phone when he heard a dial tone. Director Connor didn't want to admit he needed help from the Captain but the Director would come back once he realized he did.

***

Robert kept a watch on the front door as more police and FBI continued to flow through the wooded areas around the hospital. He wanted to call Captain

101

Kendall again but held off. The captain was probably busy coordinated this search and he didn't want to curtail him in any way. The most important thing was to find and capture Sage.

What Robert didn't know was later that same night Sage going to be in more trouble than he could ever imagine.

CHAPTER ELEVEN

Sage tried to move but realized he couldn't feel his legs. His whole body was sticky with his own blood. The bear had knocked the knife out of his hand and clawed his face and the length of his body causing rivulets of blood to flow. He had passed out from the pain a number of times as the bear continued to chew on his legs and stomach. He didn't know how he was still alive.

He somehow rolled over onto his stomach and used his right hand, the only one that had not been clawed, to pull himself along the ground by grabbing onto the dirt and roots of trees. He had to get to the road for help. His only concern now was to survive. No one would know who he was anyway. He was sure that he was unrecognizable after the mauling he had received. He began to hallucinate as the pain once again kicked up a higher notch. He cried out but quickly bit down on a stick to quiet himself for fear that the bear would return. Sage knew he wouldn't survive another attack.

***

Jeremiah and Gayle headed out to look for a place to eat. They needed to get away from the horror after the body was found near the cabin at Tambor Lake. They were told by the police after giving their statements to stay close in case they were needed for more questioning.

The teens were still quite shook up after their discovery. They sat around the now cold campfire with shocked and numb expressions. They had to endure a long session with the police since they had found the body.

The two families with children were unaware of anything happening since they had gone off early to dinner at a local diner nearby before the body was found. When they returned they had to answer questions too. The police let them go once they realized they had children who were quite upset over all the noise and activity as the police swarmed the area. They were asked to check in with the police after they settled in another area close by.

Jeremiah was worried about his wife. Gayle didn't appear to know what was going on. She looked around at the area not really seeing all the unusual activity. Jeremiah had asked the police to allow him and his wife to go look for a place to eat away from the craziness.

"I don't see the harm in you going to dinner. Your wife appears to be okay though."

Jeremiah whispered, "Well, Officer, she has early signs of Alzheimer's and is not totally aware of what is going on around her."

"Oh, I see. Sorry about that. Well, as long as you check in with us and let us know where you are going to be. We will be here most of the night."

"Thank you, Officer. We will be back after dinner. I think it is best if I take Gayle away from here for a little while."

Jeremiah led Gayle to their car and buckled her in. She appeared to be in a stupor. He smoothed the hair away from her face and kissed her soft cheek.

She smiled up at him and then looked down, her facial expression once again becoming blank.

He knew time was racing forward with the disease. He tried to focus and started the car as he pulled out of the parking lot and headed back on the road. The other visitors had told him about a small diner with a gas station about an hour or so away that had great burgers and fries. His stomach began to growl as he headed in a northerly direction.

As Jeremiah drove along, he had an hour to think over what he would have to do once he brought his wife home. He would need help taking care of her soon.

The diner came into view and he pulled into the gas station first to fill up. He looked over at Gayle but she seemed to be in her own world looking around. He patted her hand. "Honey, I need to fill up the tank and then we will go get a bite to eat in the diner. Stay put. I'll be right back." Gayle didn't seem to register anything he told her, but she did nod slightly which confused him.

Jeremiah pulled away from the pump and parked closer to the diner. He unbuckled his belt, then his wife's and led her into the diner.

There were a few other patrons but the waitress came over to them quickly to seat them and left menus with the promise she would be right back. Jeremiah noticed the diner's hours. They closed at 7:00 pm. It was now 6:00 pm.

Jeremiah smiled at the sight of this odd-looking waitress. She looked weary and disheveled with low-hanging breasts and nylons rolled down over puffy ankles. He looked over at his lovely wife and felt fortunate that she had always taken care of her appearance. He sighed knowing that soon she would no longer be able to do this.

He scanned the menu and turned to Gayle. "What do you want to eat, sweetheart?"

She didn't answer but turned to look at him and sighed. "Where are we, Jeremiah? I want to go home."

"Oh sweetheart, we are at Tambor Lake. This is where you wanted to go for the weekend. We went boating around the Lake earlier today and now we are out having dinner. What would you like to eat?" Jeremiah could feel tears threatening to fall as he looked with love at Gayle.

"I know you love burgers and fries. I will get you a cheeseburger and fries and a cup of tea. Okay?"

He waved at the bedraggled waitress as he put down the menus and prepared to order. He would get a burger too and a strong cup of coffee to keep him awake. He felt it was going to be a long night with the police investigation and Gayle's present status.

The waitress took their orders and hurried back to the kitchen. She soon came back with waters and tea and coffee. "Your burgers will be out soon. Is there anything else I can get you?"

"No, that will be all for now, thank you." Jeremiah turned toward his wife and put his arm around her slim shoulders. She looked up and smiled.

"Jeremiah, you are getting frisky, dear!" She exclaimed giddily.

He looked at her in amazement. He never knew when she would become lucid or forgetful or completely catatonic. He chuckled at hearing her voice and the humor that was evident in it.

***

Sage passed out once again as he tried to pull his body along the wooded area. He continued to make slow progress by gripping onto the base of small trees with his good hand. He couldn't feel his legs but was aware of pain in his abdomen where the bear had taken a chunk out of him. He knew he was bleeding heavily and didn't have much time before he could possibly bleed to death. He had to try to keep awake until he could get to the road. Once he got to the hill overlooking the road he could roll down and hopefully someone would see him and not run over him.

***

Jeremiah and Gayle finished their burgers which they found to be delicious. Even Gayle mentioned how good the food was. Then she once again became quiet.

He left a good tip for the waitress after paying and guided his wife back to the car. Once he had her situated in the car with her belt safely fastened she turned to him and abruptly announced, "Jerry, I want to go for a ride before we go back to the cabin. I want to see some more foliage. The colors are so beautiful. They take my breath away."

He leaned over, kissed his wife on the lips and smiled. "Of course, dear. We can take a little drive up to the next lake so you can enjoy the beauty while there is still some light. Then we'll head back. It'll be dark by then and you won't be able to see much."

Tears prickled at the inside corners of his eyes as he brushed them away and drove on to please his wife. He enjoyed these rare moments of lucidity and would do anything to make his wife happy for as long as he could.

He drove and drove and finally slowed down. There was a dark lump in the road ahead. He thought it could be an animal. It appeared to be bloody. Probably was hit by a car. He moved over to the side of the road to get a closer look. He told his wife he would be right back once he checked out what it was.

What Jeremiah didn't realize was his wife was close on his heels as he moved toward the bloody object in the road. Before he could react, he heard a blood curdling scream in his ear from Gayle who was leaning over him and looking at the thing in the road.

CHAPTER TWELVE

Mariah couldn't sleep. It was only three am. She had been tossing and turning all night. She grabbed her robe and went out to the front desk to talk to Dan and the police on guard for any news of Sage's whereabouts.

Robert was slumped forward with his head supported by his hands. He was asleep. Dan was nowhere in sight.

Mariah didn't want to wake Uncle Robert but felt compelled to do something. She gently shook his arm and whispered, "Uncle Robert, why don't you get some rest. I will take over here for you. I couldn't sleep anyway."

"What…Mariah, what are you doing up? You should be sleeping."

"No, I need to keep busy. I can't sleep. All I can think about is Sage and where he could be hiding."

"Yes, Mishy, I know." (Robert always called Mariah by a nickname of her middle name, Michelle, since she was a baby.) "I didn't realize I had fallen asleep. I was hoping to hear back from

Captain Kendall about whether they found Sage or have clues about where he could be."

"Uncle Robert I think it is time you called me Mariah. I am no longer a little girl."

"Okay, Mariah. I think it is too. Sorry about that."

"That's okay, Uncle. They can't hold us here forever, can they, Uncle Robert?"

"Well, not legally. But we could be here for another day or two. I think Sage is hiding out in the open. He wants to be close to watch our next move. Then he will strike."

"He is expecting us to stay here. Why don't we all move away from here. He will never know where we are. You know he will come back."

"He could come back here. But somehow I think he will be patient and wait for us to let down our guard. It could be days, weeks, months or maybe a year."

"Oh God, you really believe that, Uncle Robert? What would he be doing all that time if he waited a year?"

"I hate to say it but…killing. He would be killing some unsuspecting people to keep his skills fresh. The fact is, Mariah, Sage loves to kill. He loves the hunt, the torment of his victims and most of all the feeling he gets from actually committing the crime. He is one sick individual. I only wish my parents hadn't adopted him in the first place without knowing his family history."

"Do you think that would have made a difference, Uncle Robert?"

"Maybe it would have to my mother. My father, not so much. He was loving, caring and always looked for the good in people. He never suspected that Sage was anything but good. He believed that he could bring out the best in Sage if he brought him up instead of letting his mother put him in a foster home or orphanage."

"Uncle Robert! You make Gram sound like a cold-hearted person compared to Gramps. She's not! I do feel badly that I didn't get to meet Gramps though."

"You would have loved my dad and he would have loved you too. Oh, Mariah, sweetheart! I never meant to infer that my mother was anything but a good and kind person. After all, she did all she could to help Sage. He didn't want any help. He was already too far gone and no one could have helped him. He had insanity in his genes. No one is to blame for that."

"Of course she is! I love Gram. She has been wonderful to me since I was a baby, taking care of me and keeping my parents from going over the edge when they lost my twin brother. As for Uncle Sage, well…I really don't know him. I don't want to think of him as my uncle…especially after what he has done."

"Yes, that was a sad time for all of us. But thank God we have you!" Robert smiled as he took Mariah's hand in his and squeezed it.

"I don't blame you for feeling that way about Sage. I don't think of him as my brother either."

Detectives Snyder's and Armano's radios crackled to life making both Robert and Mariah stop their discussion mid-stream to listen.

Robert jumped up from the desk and walked over to Detective Armano to find out what was happening.

"Excuse me, Detective, but what's going on? Did they find anything or where Sage could be?"

"Umm, well, I can't say at this time. I'm sure Captain Kendall will get in touch with you as soon as he knows more. For now, we are only doing our job."

"Yes, of course, Detective. I appreciate all that you are doing to keep us safe. But if they don't find Sage soon, we will all go crazy. We need to get our lives back in order."

***

Later that evening the police called for a helicopter to move the severely injured body of a man to a hospital in New York City. They didn't expect this man to live. It was incredible that he had survived at all by the looks of his extensive injuries. He had been severely mauled. The claw marks and bite marks were indicative of a large bear.

The police canvassed the area and looked over the man's tent and supplies for some form of ID. All they found were some rabbit skins drying inside the tent and more traps and guns – everything that a hunter would need. They were going to go back to the precinct and look for any missing person's reports. Someone could be looking for him.

Captain Kendall heard the latest report of a bear mauling on a hunter. He didn't think too much on this since there was no connection between the man he was looking for and this hunter. Reports stated that the man was not expected to live. But he would keep tabs on the man's outcome in case he was able to tell them anything at all about seeing Sage. That's if, the injured man ever regained consciousness.

Captain sent his men in wider circles looking for Sage. He knew he would be hearing from Director Connor again if Director didn't find any clues to where Sage headed.

***

New York Medical Hospital was given the heads up that there was a severely injured patient being flown there. When the man arrived they hadn't expected him to be this badly mauled and still breathing. His body was completely covered with claw and bite marks except for his right hand and arm. With these horrific injuries the man would never look normal again. There was not much they could do beyond patching him up and trying to keep him alive until he healed well enough to have an enormous amount of plastic surgery.

Sage didn't wake up through all the triage being done on his body. After the initial surgery and heavy sedation, he would be in a coma for several months. The doctors expected to perform many more surgeries over the coming months. His body was fighting infections and would never be the same in looks or strength. He had lost chunks of his thighs, stomach and chest luckily not hitting vital organs. He was receiving donor's blood. More would be needed over the next several days to replace what Sage had lost.

He was being treated as a John Doe since there was no identification on his body or in the area where he was found. Police would be actively looking through missing person reports in case he was one of those who were missing. The Jeep that Sage had taken from Camp Tambor was stolen by two teens hiking in the area and therefore never connected to Camp Tambor and the injured man.

The authorities resumed their search for Sage elsewhere. No connection was made between the injured man and the murderer at large yet.

***

Captain Kendall's men were now searching a fifty-mile radius without any luck. It appeared that Sage had left the area without a trace. If he was still in the vicinity he must be underground, thought Captain Kendall.

He planned to have a meeting of all his men the following morning to collect information, clues and discuss the next moves. He thought it was time to let Dr. Fontana and his family go back to their lives. He would still want to circulate his men around the hospital but not as often.

***

Robert convinced Mariah to go back to bed by telling her, "Listen Mariah, I need to call the Captain again and get an update. I sense that there is more going on than these detectives want to share. Maybe Captain Kendall will tell me something. I'll let you all know what I find out in a few hours. Now go get some rest."

"Okay, Uncle Robert, but you promise to rest too. You look exhausted. You still have patients to take care of and shouldn't be neglecting them for us. We can all take care of ourselves."

"I will, Mariah, I promise. Now off you go," Robert waved her away as he picked up the desk phone and dialed the precinct.

Captain Kendall answered the call himself since he was alone in his office and had sent his secretary home hours ago. Every available officer was out searching for Sage.

"Oh, hello, Dr. Fontana. Yes, we have had an interesting night but still no sign of your brother."

"I see. But have you found out anything to suggest he could still be around here or has he left the area?"

"That's hard to say, Doctor. I can't share any of this investigation with you until I have news of his whereabouts. Then and only then will I share that with you. For now, I will be calling a meeting with my men in a few hours to move ahead with new plans. I was going to call you to let you know that we will be pulling the two detectives off duty at your hospital and letting all of you go on with your daily lives. We can't keep you holed up there forever. It looks like Sage is not coming back for now. If you see or hear anything to the contrary please let me know immediately."

"Are you sure about him not coming back here? What if he does? I can't protect my whole family by myself if they are scattered around."

"I understand, Dr. Fontana. I can ask the respective police departments in the areas to send a car around to your family's homes for a few more days to check on them but after that..."

"After that we are on our own. Is that what you are trying to say, Captain?"

"Listen, Doctor. We will do whatever we can to protect you all. There is more work to do in this case that I can't share with you. Once we have more information on things...I will know more about Sage and his whereabouts. If he were anywhere near here we would have found him already."

"You really don't know my brother or what he is capable of doing."

"Oh, I think I do, Doctor. I think I do. You sound exhausted. I think after a few more hours of sleep you will understand where I stand. Good night and give my best to your family. Tell them we will be watching their backs. Also, Doctor, please tell them that they will need to keep in touch with me especially if they see or hear from Sage in any way, shape, or form such as letters, phone calls, etc."

"Okay. You're right, I am worn-out, Captain. I'm sure you think you are doing all that you possibly can to protect us but I don't know if that is enough. I will tell my family. Good night, Captain."

***

Mariah had not gone back to bed but had knocked on Tony's door to talk to him. When Tony opened his door Mariah walked in. "Tony, I'm worried about Uncle Robert. He is trying to protect us. He's taking on too much. He has got to let the police handle it."

"Now look who is worrying? Mariah, you are trying to do the same thing. The police will handle things. They will find Sage. Give them a chance. He's a slippery guy. I know. I chased him down too. But he can't hide forever. He will come out of hiding eventually."

"Yeah, that is what I am afraid of. He will come after Uncle Robert first, then the rest of us. We may not be able to stop him, nor will the police."

"Mariah, please go back to bed. We all need to rest. It's still too early – only 3:00 a.m. We may have some news in a few hours. The police are working with the FBI on this case. They know what they are doing."

"I hope so, Tony. I truly hope so. Good night."

They kissed and went their separate ways unaware of what had been discussed by Robert and Captain Kendall. Most of all, they did not know about Sage's plight earlier that night that would keep him out of commission for a long time.

CHAPTER THIRTEEN

Jeremiah held Gayle who was hysterical from the shock she received seeing the body of the injured man. The shock actually brought her back to reality. He wished he had known she was following close behind him when he went to investigate what was in the road. It was a horrendous sight. He couldn't get it out of his mind either.

They had nothing to add to the investigation since they didn't know the man that was found. Jeremiah explained to the police about the man they met and thought was the manager. Once the Somerset Police Force finished asking them questions about the man, Jeremiah took Gayle back to the cabin and settled her in bed.

Jeremiah gave Gayle a cup of tea that he had made in the manager's office and laid down next to her. He was still shaken. He didn't realize how dangerous it could be in the woods. He planned to take his wife back home where it was safer and get some help for her condition.

Since they had been at the lake, a body was found on the premises then another body turned up on the road. He never imagined spending time at a cabin on a lake would be so perilous. He planned to pack up in the morning. If the police didn't need any more statements from him, he would leave and return to the safety of city life.

***

The following morning the police were finished with the area but still kept the grave site cordoned off. Visitors were advised they could leave, however, the police asked to be notified should they go out of state. Most of the visitors were from out of state so they had to leave their home addresses and phone numbers with the police before they left.

The teens were happy to pack up and leave in the morning as were the two families with children. The families stayed away during the police investigation and kept their children busy at area attractions until the body was taken away.

The cabins were now going to be locked and closed off since the manager's body had been discovered. Much discussion had ensued when everyone realized that the man who they thought was the manager was an imposter. The police had taken his description and searched thoroughly for any signs of this imposter to no avail.

Captain Kendall was informed of this situation by the Somerset Police Department because of the APB that had gone out for Sage. The Cadillac was connected to Anna Forster who was murdered in Lindan, New York. The police in both precincts were still hopeful that both murders would be connected somehow to Sage.

Captain Kendall called Director Connor to fill him in about the newest murder. They were both of the impression that the imposter could have been Sage. They were still at a roadblock about where he could have gone since there didn't appear to be any sign of him in the area around this lake or beyond into the other surrounding lakes.

This investigation would be a long and tedious one and would cause many sleepless nights for both the police and the FBI. Only one person would be sleeping soundly. He was unaware of all the problems he was causing for he was in a coma.

CHAPTER FOURTEEN

Morning came and hospital staff and several of the visitors at Darien Roberts Psychiatric Hospital were up and about early. Dr. Fontana and Dr. Harper did their rounds and came down to the dining room to greet those who were having breakfast.

Robert announced to his family and staff, "Good morning, everyone. I hope you all slept well. I have some good news and bad news to report. The good news is that you are now able to go back to your lives and leave any time you want. The bad news is that Sage has not been caught yet. Captain Kendall spoke with me very early this morning to report that there is no sign of Sage.

The police and FBI will continue to search and widen the search. But for now, Captain feels that we are safe to leave. He does want us to keep in touch and report if we see or hear from Sage in any way, letters, calls, etc."

"Uncle Robert, what do you think about all this? Do you think Sage is still nearby, waiting to pounce on us?" Mariah held onto Tony's hand as she waited for her uncle's response.

"Well, Mariah, yes, I think Sage is nearby. I believe he is waiting for the police and FBI to get weary of searching for him. He is a cagey fellow, smarter than we are about such things. But I also think that it is time for us to get on with our lives. We must be vigilant but not afraid to live each day and continue to do the things we want and need to do."

Robert observed the faces of his family when he completed his speech as such. He was waiting for any other reactions to come forth.

His mother was the first to speak. "Robert, we are not afraid of Sage. He should be afraid of us. We are a tight-knit family and he is jealous of that. He never felt like a part of this family and will never be."

"I expected you to say that, Mother. You are a force to be reckoned with," Robert chuckled at his mother's bravado.

Ronald smiled and added, "You know your mother, Robert. She is one tough lady. I should know. She is my boss and keeps me in line. Please don't worry about her. I will be close by to make sure she is protected."

"Now Ronald, you should not feel like you have to protect me. I am capable of taking care of myself. I have done well for many years since my husband died."

"Yes, dear lady, that I know. But humor me a little and let me do my part. My father would expect nothing less of me."

"Ah, so that is where this urgency to care for me is coming from. Your father was an honorable and caring man. I miss him. You are like him in so many ways, Ronald. He would have been proud to see the man you have become."

"Thank you, Ma'am!"

Robert's sister and her husband responded in kind, "Listen Robert, we are not children. Please do not treat us as such. We can take care of ourselves and go back to our lives. We only need to keep in close touch to ensure that we are all safe."

"Betsy, you know I will keep in contact with all of you. I would feel better if you stayed with Mother though. It would be easier and safer for you to be together. With the large house Mother has, there is plenty of room for all of you – you too, Mariah!"

"Yes, Mariah! Why don't you come to stay with me? Tony there is room for you too."

"Well, I don't know yet, Gram. I plan to go back to college. Tony has a job at the college he can go back to. We will be together there on campus. We can watch over each other, right, Tony?" Mariah smiled and squeezed Tony's hand.

"Oh, sure, okay. That sounds good. I'm happy to hear that you're going to complete your degree, Mariah. I was worried that you wouldn't want to go back there with all the bad memories."

"They are all behind me now, Tony. I've worked them out in my mind. I doubt that Sage will go there. There is no reason for him to return. He is well known by the police and they will be keeping a lookout for him."

"Yes, I agree, Mariah. Do you need a ride back to the college to sign up? I need to phone the director and let him know that I will be back. I left quite unexpectedly but my absence was necessary. I needed to protect you."

"That's wonderful, Mariah. It will do you good to get back to school and engross yourself in your studies. I will contact the college and let them know what has transpired so they will be aware of Sage being on the loose again," Robert responded with some worry evident in his voice.

"Oh, Mariah, are you sure you want to do that, honey?" Mariah's mother and father voiced their concern.

"You knew that I would be leaving the nest soon. I had planned to get my own apartment right after college. I may as well get it sooner. Don't you think so, Tony?"

"Huh, what did you say, Mariah?" Tony looked shaken about this unexpected news.

"We could get an apartment together off campus. Then my parents wouldn't worry so much about me. You will be there to keep me company. We can watch over each other," Mariah explained clearly happy with her newfound plans.

"Um, well, I guess that would work. Yes, sounds like a good idea if that is okay with your parents." Tony looked expectantly at Betsy and Frank Hampton for any sign of acceptance. He had wanted to do that after Mariah graduated but now was as good a time to make the move especially with Sage still on the loose.

"Okay, then it is settled, right Mom and Dad?"

Betsy and Frank exchanged questioning looks then nodded in unison. They appeared happy that Mariah would be looked after further away from home.

Beatrice spoke up and addressed the happy couple, "Hey, you two lovebirds. I want to pay for your apartment while Mariah is still in college. It would be one less expense for you to think about. I also will give you some money for your first semester, books, etc. Once Tony is making some money then you can take over the payments. Will that work for you?"

"Wow, Gram that is too generous of you! Thank you!" Mariah walked over to where her gray-haired but young-looking grandmother was sitting and hugged her in gratitude.

Tony was quiet as he waited for Mariah to sit down again. Directing his response to Beatrice, "I don't mind you helping us out but I want to take care of Mariah once I am back to work. Don't get me wrong, I appreciate your help. I would be crazy not to."

"I understand, Tony. You are an honorable man. I won't interfere once you tell me you are working and receiving a pay. I want to take care of my granddaughter. Humor this old woman," Beatrice pleaded.

"All right, Mrs. Fontana, but only for the first semester. That is kind and most generous of you."

Mariah turned toward Tony, kissed him on the cheek and whispered in his ear, "Thank you, Tony!"

Once everyone finished their coffee and gathered what little belongings they had Ronald escorted them to the limo. Robert followed them out to the parking lot.

"Thank you Robert, for taking us in. Appreciate the wonderful dinner and breakfast. Compliments to the chef," Ronald expressed for all concerned.

"Oh, here's Miguel. You can all thank him yourselves."

Miguel shook hands, with the men and hugged the ladies as they expressed their appreciation for his cooking skills.

"It was my pleasure to serve all of you. This is what a chef lives for – people who love his food! Thank you!"

Beatrice hugged Miguel a little longer than everyone else for she was whispering in his ear, "If

Robert ever gives you a hard time, you're always welcome at my house. I could use a chef like you!"

"Oh, thank you, Mrs. Fontana. It would be a pleasure to serve you but I am in Robert's debt for all he has done for me. I could never leave him. Who would take care of him?"

"I understand, Miguel. But what Robert needs is a good woman and you too!"

"Yeah, when you find two, let us know!" Miguel laughed as he headed back to the hospital to check on his staff and then send them home to rest.

Robert bid his goodbyes to his family next and reminded them what Captain Kendall mentioned about keeping in touch.

"Don't forget to call me when you arrive home. I need to hear from all of you daily until Sage is found. If I don't hear from you every day I will call you. That goes for you, Mariah and Tony!"

"Yes, Uncle Robert. We'll call to check up on you too!" Mariah retorted as she and Tony got into her car.

Ronald started the limo's engine and pulled away as they all waved one last time.

***

Things were not going as smoothly for Sage. He had to undergo more surgery.

CHAPTER FIFTEEN

Captain Kendall looked over his notes about the injured man found in the road in the lakes region.

He had requested that the hospital contact his office as soon as the patient regained consciousness and was able to talk about his ordeal. So far the man had endured dozens of surgeries but hadn't come out of a coma.

Captain was also keeping his men on alert about Sage who was still at large. It was bizarre that he disappeared after the bodies of Anna Forster, her dog and the Camp Manager were found.

It was possible that Sage wanted to lay low for the time being until the police and FBI gave up on finding him. *What Sage doesn't know is, I will never give up!* Captain Kendall thought.

FBI Director Connor had not found any connection between the murders and Sage. No fibers, hairs or anything was detected. It appeared that the hands were bleached, reason why no DNA was detected under the nails. Sage, if he did commit these murders, was a careful man or maybe lucky.

The police and the FBI had reluctantly joined forces and compared notes between their offices and departments including forensics. They both believed that Sage had been responsible for the murders and wouldn't give up trying to make the connection. One day soon they would get lucky.

***

The six teens traveled to some of the other lakes after the murder at Tambor Lake. They didn't want to go home yet and visited and stayed in other cabins on the lakes around the area for a couple more days. They had taken some time off from school and would go back for the next semester.

The murder had shaken them all up and they were even more shaken when they heard about the man who had been mauled by a bear. This mauling had finally made them decide to go home. They packed up and went back to college and their lives once again.

After being back at college and doing mundane things several months later the boys realized that they were getting low on cash. They remembered the ring that they had found in the pseudo-manager's cabin. It could bring them some much needed funds. They decided to look for a pawn shop in the town around their campus and see what they could get for it.

***

Mrs. Kilgardy cleaned out her mother's house in preparation for its selling. She still couldn't believe her mother had been murdered. Why anyone would kill a harmless old lady was beyond comprehension. Mrs. Kilgardy shook her head and cleared her thoughts. There was much work to be done and finding her mother's ring was a priority.

Her mother hadn't left behind much for her family to have as a remembrance, except her wedding ring. Mrs. Kilgardy knew her mother never took it off. She feared whoever had killed her might have stolen it

It had been a difficult time for Mrs. Kilgardy and her family when they had to bury her mother. Anna Forster could be a cantankerous soul but she had a good heart. The dog had taken the place in Anna's heart of her deceased husband. They were always together. It was fitting that they died together and were laid to rest side by side. That is what her mother would have wanted.

Mrs. Kilgardy had spoken to Captain Kendall many times over the past several months after her mother's death. He had promised to contact her if he ever found her mother's killer and her ring. Mrs. Kilgardy hadn't heard from him for a while and decided to check in to see if there was any news as to who killed her mother and stole her ring.

Captain Kendall took the call from Mrs. Kilgardy. *I wonder what she wants after all this time.*

"Hello, Mrs. Kilgardy. How are you doing?"

"Hello, Captain. I'm okay. Sorry to bother you. I'm sure you're a busy man and I don't want to take up too much of your time. But…I have looked everywhere and still haven't found my mother's ring. I fear that someone must have stolen it after they killed her. It really wasn't worth much but it meant more than anything else my mother ever received from my father. She never would have taken it off. Do you have any leads as to who murdered my mother? She never hurt anyone. I don't understand who would want to do this!"

"I understand, Mrs. Kilgardy. We don't have any leads about her killer or her ring at this time but I promise to keep a lookout for it. It is bound to turn up if someone stole it. I will have my men check all the pawn shops around the area and see if it turns up. I promise also to call you as soon as we know who was responsible for your mother's death. Can you give me a description of the ring?"

"Yes, it was what you call a waterfall ring. All the diamonds are in a row like a waterfall. Thank you, Captain. I appreciate whatever you can do. I hope to hear from you soon."

"You're welcome, Mrs. Kilgardy. I'll do my best."

Captain Kendall called a meeting of his men after the first shift to fill them in about the missing ring. He didn't want to admit that he had forgotten about it. With some luck it could be a connection to the killer of the old woman.

"Listen men, it seems that the old woman who was killed with her dog had a wedding ring which was not on her body. Her daughter called to tell me that she has not found it anywhere in her mother's house. She indicated that it's called a waterfall ring, whatever that is. I want all of you to check pawn shops around the lakes and within a fifty mile radius. If no luck, then expand the search. I want that ring found. It could be the connection we need to Sage."

There were "yes sirs" all around the room as the officers, drained and edgy from all the overtime the past several months, wanted to go home to bed. They knew how tenacious their captain was. The officers went back to their desks and searched for pawn shops first within fifty miles then beyond. They left messages with the pawn shops to keep a look out for a wedding ring. They told them to call about any wedding ring since they didn't have a solid description of it. None of them knew what a waterfall ring looked like. But the pawn shops would probably know. As soon as the last pawn shop was called, the men headed home. Now the waiting would begin.

***

The teens visited a pawn shop a few blocks from college and asked the manager what he would give them for the ring.

"Listen, kids, this isn't worth much. I can't give you more than a hundred for it. The diamonds don't look like they are good quality and are too minuscule to bring any money on resale."

The teens looked at one another and shook their heads. They didn't see any way to convince the manager to give them more. They knew nothing about diamonds either.

"No, that is not enough," Steve insisted.

"Let's go elsewhere," Reg agreed.

The teens turned to walk out of the shop when the manager called them back. "Wait a minute. Come back. I think I can do a little better than that."

The boys smiled at each other and came back to the counter placing the ring in front of the man. They waited for his response.

"Well, how much can you give us?" Steve's impatience was evident.

"Let me look at it more closely. I may have been too hasty with my evaluation."

The boys waited as the man examined the ring in more detail this time. They played along with him hoping that they would get more to split six ways.

Steve whispered to Chace and Reg, "We can split this three ways instead of six. The girls don't even know about the ring. I won't tell them if you don't."

"Hmm, maybe we could do that. As long as they don't find out. There will be hell to pay," Chace agreed.

"Heh, you bet. They would kill us!" Reg chuckled.

"Ssh, looks like he's finished with his examination of the ring. Don't say anything. Let me do the talking," Steve urged.

"Well boys, I think I may be able to give you a little more for this. The diamonds aren't too bad after all under closer scrutiny." The pawn shop owner wanted the ring when he noticed that the band was platinum which was peculiar on such a small ring and the diamonds were of excellent quality though small. He didn't want the boys to know that the ring was worth more than he originally told them.

The boys were anxious to get this deal over with. They knew that they could be in big trouble if anyone went looking for the ring. They wanted to take the money and hightail it out of there.

"How does $450 sound?" The manager knew he had the boys when their faces took on a look of triumph at the higher price. He would still be able to sell it for $650 but these boys wouldn't know that.

The boys agreed readily and grabbed the cash and walked out of the shop as quickly as they could in case the man changed his mind. They never looked back.

The police hadn't called this particular shop since it was slightly out of the fifty plus miles they had covered. But the shop manager suspected something wasn't right about these boys bringing in an old wedding ring like this. He chose not to report it and instead would sell it as soon as he could to get rid of the evidence.

A few days later a couple came in and bought the ring for their engagement for $700.

CHAPTER SIXTEEN

Mariah was finishing up her third year at Tristan College in Vermont taking advanced classes and doubling up on courses to finish earlier. She felt she had to make up for lost time thanks to all the craziness she had endured. She wanted to put it all behind her.

Tony had found a cute little apartment for them to live while she finished up her degree and he worked as a dean of students on campus. Her grandmother had paid for the first few months' rent on the apartment in order for them to get on their feet.

Mariah took on a part-time job at the dress shop off campus where she had previously worked on the weekends to help out. They planned on paying back her grandmother for the loan. Mariah knew that Gram would fight her and not want to take it but she would try for her own self-respect.

Tony and Mariah managed to have some time to spend together at night after a quick dinner. They talked about what their life would be like once she completed her studies.

Mariah wanted to move away from the East Coast. She didn't want to be anywhere near where Sage had committed his deadly deeds. She was trying to convince her family to move away with Tony and her. So far, they didn't want to budge.

Uncle Robert had his hospital to run in New York. Her grandmother had her huge house where her mother and father were now also living in New Hampshire. They were still being protective of her and called every day or two to check on her.

Tony had spoken to them all and promised that he would keep Mariah safe. Many times on the campus he had followed Mariah around in between his own appointments to ensure she was okay. Mariah had not seen him yet. If she had, he was sure she would have given him a piece of her mind.

Mariah was an independent young woman and had matured and grown stronger with her ordeals. Tony didn't want to see her go through anything like that again. He kept in touch with Dr. Fontana who in turn stayed in touch with Captain Kendall. All three of them wanted the same thing – Sage caught and punished.

It was beginning to feel that this was not going to happen. There had been no sign of Sage since he escaped. The two murders were not connected to him according to the police and FBI. Tony didn't believe that. He still felt there was a connection. But how were they going to prove it? They would have to wait until Sage made a crucial mistake, then they would all pounce.

***

The doctors were closely monitoring Sage after yet another surgery. His vitals were good but he was still in a coma. They had to use cadaver skin to replace all the skin he had lost from the bear's attack. It would take many more surgeries to cover the area of skin that he had lost. His body was not yet rejecting any of the grafts they had previously applied. That was a good sign.

The authorities had yet to find anyone who had reported a man missing in that area of the woods surrounding the lakes region. They were still calling him a John Doe. It looked like he was a hunter who was in the wrong place at the wrong time.

As his bills mounted the hospital was in a quandary as to who to bill. There would come a time when hopefully the patient would regain consciousness and strength to tell them who he was and eventually they would receive payment. With his serious life-threatening injuries they had no choice but to do all they could to keep him alive until then.

Sage was unaware of anything going on around him as his body struggled to heal and regain control.

***

Mariah woke early for her classes after a fitful night of sleep. She had dreamt that Sage was coming to get her. She saw him moving through the campus with a knife in his hand. His face was not visible due to the darkness in her dream. She shivered as she felt him coming closer.

She knew she had to get up even if it was only 5:00 am and her first class was at 8:30 am. She tiptoed out of bed without waking Tony and dressed in her jogging pants and top. She wasn't a jogger but a fast walker. She had plenty of time to get in a couple of miles or so walking around campus, get back, shower, and have breakfast all before Tony woke up. He didn't have to be in his office until 9:00 am.

Mariah kept feeling as if someone was watching her from a distance. She walked as quickly as she could looking over her shoulder from time to time to assure herself that no one was following.

Upon completing her two miles she stopped by the coffee shop and picked up two coffees and bagels for Tony and herself. She wasn't in the mood to have a big breakfast.

When Mariah arrived back at their apartment Tony was getting up and preparing to get into the shower. She called out to him, "Good morning, Tony. I've got breakfast. Come on out after you finish and eat with me."

Tony yelled back, "Be there in a few."

"Where did you go so early this morning, Mariah?" Tony asked as he came into their neat but small kitchen.

"I went for a walk. Couldn't sleep much last night. Kept having a dream about…you know who. I saw him coming after me with a knife but I couldn't see his face. It was obscured by the darkness."

"Oh, Mariah, honey. You need to relax. Sage is not coming back here. He doesn't even know where you are. Besides, I am here to watch over you. I promised that I would take care of you and I always keep my promises. You know that, don't you?" Tony put his arm around Mariah after settling next to her on the stool in front of their small island.

"I know, Tony. I know. But what do you think it means that I can't see his face. Maybe my mind has erased it somehow. I can't remember what he looked like. How could I forget that?"

"I don't know, Mariah. Maybe it's your mind's way of protecting you from the previous trauma. Try not to think about him. Keep your mind occupied with your studies. Let Captain Kendall handle Sage. He will contact Dr. Fontana once he finds him. Your uncle will call us as soon as he hears that his brother has been caught. It is all a matter of time…hopefully a short time. Sage will make a mistake and that is when he will be found."

"I hope so, Tony. I really hope so," Mariah sighed and finished up her breakfast and headed for the shower. A half hour later she grabbed her bag and books, and bent down and kissed Tony soundly on the lips before leaving the apartment.

Tony called after her, "Don't forget to call me when you finish your classes around lunch time so we can eat together in the café. I want to try that new sub they advertised yesterday."

"Okay, Tony. You are always thinking of your stomach. See you later."

Mariah looked at her watch and checked the time and then headed to her first class, journalism. Her professor was a tough one and always called on her several times in class. She checked her hair and lipstick in her small mirror and walked into the building behind several of her classmates.

Professor Gyropolos was writing on the board and turned to face the class. There were roughly 100 students in this auditorium-style class. The professor scanned the classroom and centered on Mariah as always. She busied herself with her backpack and pulled out her book, pad and pencil.

Mariah could feel his eyes studying her every move. His attention freaked her out. What was up with him? He reminded her of someone else. She hated to even think his name – Sage. She studied him in between checking her notes as he continued to stare at her. He had curly brown hair that was graying, a short beard and mustache, intense dark brown eyes, and was probably in his forties or early fifties.

What Mariah didn't know was Mr. Gyropolos was an avid follower of serial killers like Sage. He thought of himself as a student learning his craft – killing. Professor had already killed one student a year ago. No one ever connected him to the crime.

In fact the body was found mutilated in a similar way to Sage's work. The police blamed the murder on Sage even though Sage was nowhere near the area when the girl was murdered.

Mariah shivered even though she wasn't cold. She buried her face in her book to keep his eyes off of her. She couldn't stand his close scrutiny of her each day. She would have to change professors. He was becoming unnerving to be around. She couldn't take another day of him of the rest of this semester.

Mariah answered a few questions the Professor directed at her and jumped up when the professor dismissed the class. She looked at her watch and noticed she had some time, before she was to meet Tony for lunch, to go to the office and request a change in instructors for this class.

Professor Gyropolos watched Mariah leave. He could feel his skin jumping with anticipation. Soon he would find a way to get to Mariah. She would be perfect. He looked forward to getting up close and personal with her. He hadn't heard where Sage had gone. He was missing. Where could he have gone? He had watched Sage in action from afar and admired him for his skills. He knew he was ready to follow in Sage's footsteps and who better than Mariah for his next victim.

CHAPTER SEVENTEEN

Tony waited in the café for Mariah. She was already ten minutes late and hadn't called to say why. He was getting anxious. Where could she be? She had finished her morning classes and didn't have an afternoon class until 2:00 pm.

Tony sipped his coffee and looked up as Mariah came into the room and hurried over to his table. He could see by her face that she was upset. He waited patiently, while she settled down, for an explanation.

Mariah sighed and explained, "Sorry I'm late. I had to go to the office to change my Journalism class. I can't take seeing Professor Gyropolos another minute. He creeps me out. He stares at me throughout the class. I am the only one he calls on. Everyone notices it too. They think I am teacher's pet. I think he is a little crazy if you ask me. He reminds me of…you know who. I can't be in his class another minute."

Tony listened and looked kindly on Mariah. "Sweetheart, I'm sure he isn't at all like Sage. There's only one of him, thank God. Did you get to change classes?" Tony observed Mariah's countenance as he paused for her answer.

"Um, well, finally I managed to convince the secretary to make a change. It's effective tomorrow. I know I will enjoy the class with Professor Jonas. I heard she is creative and makes the class fun and interesting. I need a light-hearted professor for a change.

Tony smiled and tried to make light of the situation but he felt anxious about this professor. He had seen him on campus and in the staff lounge on more than one occasion. He felt the same way as Mariah – the man was more than a little eccentric. He would make time to keep an eye on Professor Gyropolos.

"What would you like to eat, Mariah? I waited for you to begin. I only picked up some coffee."

Mariah stared off into the distance and appeared not to hear Tony.

He repeated himself, "Mariah, what would you like to have for lunch? I can get it for you, honey."

"Huh, oh, sorry, I'm not too hungry. I'll have a salad."

"Okay, honey, I'll get it for you."

Tony moved over to the salad bar and filled a container and chose a dressing on the side for Mariah. He added some protein – chicken, cheese, salami to round off her meal. For himself he picked up a meatball sub and a water for each of them.

Mariah stared off into space as Tony placed her lunch in front of her. He gently tapped her on the shoulder. "Mariah, here's your lunch. You need to eat before your next class."

"Okay, Tony. Please don't worry about me. I'm fine. I was thinking of Sage and wondering what he's been doing and where he's been hiding all this time. It's not like him to not nose around. I'm sure he knows where we are by now. I hope he isn't bothering anyone else in my family. Maybe I should call Uncle Robert or my grandmother and parents. They could have heard about Sage."

"I'm sure we would have heard by now if Sage had been found. It's probably because he is still in hiding."

"Yeah, Tony, I guess you're right. He is a sneaky guy. It's funny – peculiar kind of funny, I mean, that he hasn't committed any more murders. What could he possibly be doing?"

Tony hesitated then went on, "I thought it's quite probable that he got injured and is hunkered down somewhere healing."

"Well, whatever it is, I am relieved that he hasn't hurt anyone else, that we know of, that is." Mariah sighed.

Tony was more intuitive than he realized but he would need his intuitiveness to deal with more problems ahead to keep Mariah safe.

***

On the next scheduled Journalism class, Professor Gyropolos waited for the class to fill up. He kept his eyes peeled for Mariah. The last student entered and closed the door. He scanned the classroom once again but could not find Mariah. Maybe she was late or sick. He couldn't wait any longer to begin his lecture. He turned toward the board and wrote the outline for his speech.

Mariah sat in Professor Jonas' class and pulled out her notebook and pen and prepared to take notes for the first time. She loved this professor's style and how she walked back and forth as she spoke stopping to look at each student and smile. She made the class comfortable and weird to say…safe.

Mariah realized that this was the first time she felt really safe in a classroom since she had been in college. It all began with Sage. She had the odd feeling back then that she was being watched. Now that feeling began again but not while she was in Professor Jonas' class.

She knew she had to be proactive in her own life and keep her eyes and ears open. Sage could come back any time. Mariah couldn't expect Tony to protect her every minute of the day.

After class was over, Mariah went into the shopping area outside of the campus and found a shop that carried odds and ends. In the shop she found a keychain that had a flashlight and a siren on it. Two things that could be helpful in case she needed to protect herself. The flashlight which was quite bright would blind a perpetrator long enough for her to escape while the siren would attract attention and also deter anyone from attacking her.

It was a sad affair when one must resort to finding ways to protect oneself. She remembered what her uncle's secretary had told her about her near escape from Sage. Sharynn had a siren and a pepper spray that had saved her life. If Sage had managed to grab

Sharynn, she would not have lived to tell anyone about him.

Mariah hurried back to the campus and went to her apartment. She wanted to talk to her uncle about any news about Sage. She was feeling insecure and needed to hear his voice. She was used to depending on him to relax her by his calming manner. He had been the one to bring her back from her state of apoplexy after the horrendous attack upon her friend, Amanda. Mariah could feel her eyes beginning to tear up at the thought of poor Amanda.

The phone rang at her uncle's hospital and Mariah waited for his secretary, Sharynn, to pick up. When Mariah heard Sharynn's voice, she relaxed visibly, "Hi Sharynn, it's Mariah. How are you? Is my uncle around? I couldn't reach him on his cell."

"Oh hi, Mariah. He must have silenced his cell to do his rounds. Everything is pretty quiet here. How are you doing?"

"I'm okay, Sharynn."

"That's good. Your uncle is still making rounds, but I'll call him and let him know you are on the line. Can you hold for a minute?"

"Thanks, Sharynn. Sure."

Mariah tapped her nails on the table and swung her right leg over her left as she waited for Uncle Robert to come on the line.

"Mariah, how are you, sweetie? I was thinking about you."

"I'm fine, Uncle Robert. I...needed to hear your voice. I got so used to hearing your voice when I was in therapy that I miss talking with you, especially when I'm upset."

"What's wrong, Mariah? I can tell by your voice that something is troubling you."

"Yeah, I guess you would be the one person who could tell that. Well, a strange thing happened here at school."

Mariah told her uncle about Professor Gyropolos and his odd behavior and how it made her so uncomfortable that she had to change classes. He listened and waited until she was through with her explanation.

"Do you feel better in Professor Jonas' class now? Has Professor Gyropolos bothered you since you left his class?"

"Yes, I do feel relief being in her class. And no…he hasn't bothered me. In fact, I don't think he knows about my switching classes yet."

"I see. Well, please keep me informed if he does bother you. Did you tell Tony about this?"

"Oh yes, Tony was the first one I told. He's like you. He knows when there's a problem by the sound of my voice or by the look on my face. I tend to zone out too if I have anything on my mind."

"Good. I want you to keep Tony informed. I also want you to call me whenever you need to talk. Okay, Mariah? I'm here for you."

"Thank you, Uncle Robert. I appreciate that. I'm sorry to bother you and take you away from your patients. I forget that I am not your patient anymore."

"No problem, Mariah. I will always think of you as my special patient. Oh, Miguel was asking for you. He misses you. He asked me when you were going to visit."

"Thank you, Uncle! Tell Miguel that I will visit as soon as I have some time off. Mom and Dad have been after me, too, to visit them. I will be home for

Thanksgiving and again at Christmas. Maybe we can all get together at your place again."

"Yes, I think we could arrange that. We have enough space here to have a big celebration with turkey and all the fixings. Miguel would love to cook for us. I'll mention that to him. Now Mariah, please be careful and keep me informed. Don't walk on campus alone at night either. Okay?"

"I'd like that, Uncle Robert. Oh, don't worry. I am playing it safe. I even picked up a siren and a blinding flashlight for protection. I saw how the siren saved Sharynn."

"Smart girl! I'm relieved to hear that. Stay vigilant."

"Oh I will! Oh, Uncle Robert, did you hear anything new about Sage from the police?"

"No, nothing new. No sign of him yet. I still think he is hiding away. The detectives have long since left and no longer patrol the area. They all think that Sage has left the state. I don't think that Captain Kendall is letting this investigation slide though. He is adamant about catching Sage before the FBI."

***

Sage was still not a threat but another was preparing to follow in his footsteps.

CHAPTER EIGHTEEN

Tony was in the teacher's lounge and asking around about Professor Gyropolos. No one seemed to know anything about him. The professor had come to the college recently transferring from another college. He stayed much to himself and didn't socialize in the staff lounge.

The next step for Tony was to get friendly with the college president's secretary in order to obtain access to the staff records. He needed to look closely at Professor Gyropolos' file. He wanted to know as much as he could about this man who appeared to be interested in his Mariah.

Tony noticed how upset Mariah had been at lunch and did not want to see her regressing. She had been through enough turmoil losing her friend and nearly losing her own life when Sage had gone on his rampage at the college.

Tony had been surprised that Mariah had wanted to return to the college where it all had happened. He questioned her about it but saw how adamant she had been to overcome her fears by facing them head on. He was proud of her fearless nature but also was concerned that any one thing could trigger her to have a relapse.

Tony returned to his office to make a call to Dr. Fontana to check in on the progress by the police and FBI in finding Sage. He hadn't heard anything for a week or more now. No news, in this case, was not going to be good news.

Dr. Fontana picked up the phone himself. "Hi Tony. Is everything okay with Mariah?"

"Hi Dr. Fontana. Oh, yes for now. I should fill you in on what is happening here."

"Before you go any further, Mariah called me today and told me about the professor."

"Oh, good. What do you make of this guy? What would cause him to pick on her like that?"

"I don't know, Tony. But I would suggest you keep close tabs on him and watch over Mariah. I don't want anything to cause her to regress. The professor could only be interested in her because of what happened to her. Maybe it's a curiosity factor."

"Yeah, could be. But it's a sick one. I'm going to check out his file as soon as I can and keep an eye on him. He is a peculiar fellow. I don't feel comfortable with him on campus and anywhere near Mariah. There's something about him that I can't put my finger on yet but I will keep digging. Well, Dr. Fontana, I don't want to keep you any longer. Wanted to touch base. I'll check back again soon. If you hear anything about Sage, please let me know. You have my cell."

"Thanks, Tony. I owe you for keeping close watch on Mariah. Oh, I will definitely call you with any news about Sage. We'll celebrate when he's caught. Take care of Mariah and watch your back. Talk to you soon. Thanks again."

"No problem, Doctor. I'll do my best to take care of Mariah. Bye for now."

Tony headed over to the main office to talk to the secretary. He had some reading to do there from a file.

***

Professor Gyropolos hadn't seen Mariah in his class all week. He was beginning to worry that she was sick or maybe skipping his classes. He went to the office to check on any messages about her being too sick to attend classes.

The secretary assured the professor that she had not called in. As she scrolled over her notes she hesitated then reported, "Well, it looks like she changed classes. She is now in Professor Jonas' Journalism class."

Professor Gyropolos' anger began to rise when he heard this. *What did she think she was doing?* He did all he could to make his classes interesting and calling on her daily to keep her involved.

I guess that's not enough! Professor began to rant and rave to himself. Other staff stopped to look at him and offer their help but after he gave them a death stare they hurriedly went on their way.

The secretary tried to ignore the professor as he mumbled to himself. She could see that he was upset over the change the student had made but his mumbling was incoherent and didn't appear to make any sense. His facial expressions also frightened her. She kept her head down and did not look up until he finally moved away from her desk.

Professor Gyropolos rushed back to his office and gathered his books. He planned to stop for lunch and then go looking for Mariah. He would check Professor Jonas' schedule and plan to follow Mariah after class. He knew which apartment she was in for he had followed her after class one day. He had been keeping a close eye on her since she came back to the college. He was becoming more obsessed with Mariah every minute of the day.

***

Mariah was unaware that she was the cause of dramatic concern to the professor. She avoided him at all costs, going out of her way to not eat in the café when she knew he would be there. She also took the long way around to get to her classes that were anywhere near his room. So far the extra effort she put in was paying off.

She felt more relaxed and safe…that was what she didn't realize she needed to feel since Sage. Mariah had gotten used to being careful, always looking over her shoulder. She found that she continued to do that now but for another reason – the professor.

Sage appeared to be laying low for a while. She would stay vigilant. She knew that Tony would be there in case she needed him. Mariah worried about Tony becoming too possessive and obsessive about her safety.

She knew that she owed Tony her life and always felt safer when he was near. She wanted to finish her degree as soon as she possibly could and get away from this college and the professor.

Mariah knew that Tony was going to ask her to marry him once she received her degree. He had already talked to her parents and her uncle about this.

Mariah wasn't supposed to know that he had a talk with her family about marriage but Tony let a few things slip that led her to believe he had. She thought over the past year and a half that she had known Tony and smiled. She wanted to get married and begin a life with the man she loved. She would not let anything or anybody prevent that from happening.

Mariah hurried on her way to Professor Jonas' class. She had prepared her paper and felt confident that she would earn a high grade. She had spent a few hours going over it again and again to polish it to perfection. She loved writing and now enjoyed it more thanks to Professor Jonas who listened and appeared to care for each of her students. Nothing like Professor Gyropolos, thank God! There was something not quite right about him. He was too much like her Uncle Sage. Oh, she hated to call Sage uncle.

Mariah was zoning out and realized suddenly that she had passed her classroom and was now outside Professor Gyropolos' class. She abruptly turned around and ran back as fast as she could before Professor Gyropolos saw her.

Once Mariah settled down in her seat in the auditorium-style seating she felt better and sighed in relief. What was she thinking by not paying attention to where she was going? She would have to stop this daydreaming or it could be detrimental to her health.

What Mariah didn't realize was Professor Gyropolos had seen her outside his classroom and had followed her behind some other students as she made her way back to Professor Jonas' class. He stood outside the door and peered in spotting Mariah in the back center of the auditorium. He smiled but not in a happy way for he was still disgruntled over her changing classes. He pulled himself away from the doorway before Mariah could spot him and headed back to his own classroom. He had plans for Mariah and only needed to perfect them. In time she would be unable to get away from him. He smiled again, but this time thought of pleasant times ahead with Mariah.

***

Sage was unaware of someone taking over where he left off with his deadly deeds. He was dealing with survival. Sage's body was fighting to stay alive as he began his comeback from a deep coma.

Bells and whistles sounded as Sage's body went into spasms and yanked at his restraints. Hospital staff ran from all directions to his room in efforts to control his body from harming all the skin grafts that they had performed on him.

The doctors moved in and out of Sage's room monitoring his signs on all the machines he was hooked up to. His eyes were rapidly moving back and forth. He was dreaming.

Sage stirred restlessly as he continued to come back to consciousness. The doctors didn't want him to move his legs due to the delicate skin grafts.

Sage moaned and continued to thrash as his body realized the pain and suffering he was now feeling. Doctors and nurses tried to restrain him and finally had to inject Sage with some meds to calm him down without putting him back into a coma.

Sage finally calmed down and his eyes blinked open as they became accustomed to the bright lights of the hospital room. He looked around at his surroundings and realized where he was. A nurse was taking his blood pressure when she noticed him looking at her. She cried out for the doctor to come. "Our patient is awake, doctor! He's finally awake!"

Sage heard the urgency in the nurse's voice and wondered why she was so excited. He was not yet aware of how long he had been under a coma and what had been done to him. The nurse smiled at Sage and spoke to him in a soft soothing voice.

"You are in the hospital and have been here for nearly a year now. You have been in a coma to protect your injuries and give them time to heal. It appears that your body has decided it is time for you to wake up. You will feel a lot of pain but I have injected you with a muscle relaxant and a pain killer. These should make you comfortable without putting you back into a coma. How do you feel?"

Sage moved his mouth but nothing came out. He tried to clear it but no sound. He looked at the plain nurse, who had mousy brown hair and a long nose, and shook his head. He blinked his eyes to try and tell her he couldn't respond.

The nurse looked with sympathy at her patient and nodded. "It's okay. It may take a little while for you to get your voice back. You were injured in a bear attack. Do you remember? Your voice box was torn but we repaired it as much as we could. You may sound differently now but you should be able to speak only in a deeper tone."

Two doctors rushed into Sage's room as the nurse continued to administer to her patient and explain his condition.

"Okay, nurse, we will take it from here." Sage looked up into the faces of two men, one large with dark features and skin the tone of ebony. The other doctor was smaller with blond hair and green eyes almost the same color of someone... Sage gritted his teeth as he looked into these eyes.

Sage tried to talk once again but was unsuccessful. He shook his head and sighed.

"It's quite all right, dear boy," the ebony doctor stated in a clipped fashion evidently from England or thereabouts. "I am Dr. Rasper and this is Dr. Blaine."

The two doctors conferred as they moved away from the patient to compare notes. They reviewed the chart with the latest vitals supplied by the nurse and returned to the patient.

This time Dr. Blaine spoke. "Listen, we are going to continue to monitor your progress. You have a long road ahead of you and more surgeries to repair the damage you have incurred. Do you remember anything about what happened to you?"

Sage shook his head.

"Okay, once your vocal cords are strong enough you will be able to speak but you will sound different because of the extensive damage. I think the nurse explained a little to you about your injuries. Let me sum them up for you in common language. You sustained severe lacerations and damage across your face, neck, stomach, chest and legs. These lacerations were evidently done by a large bear. You were found in the road outside the lakes region. Your tent and supplies were found a short distance away in the woods. Are you a hunter or trapper?"

Sage shrugged his shoulders. He couldn't remember why he was there or what he did. In fact, he couldn't remember who he was. All he could remember was someone he knew had green eyes and seeing this man's eyes make him angry. This fact didn't make any sense to him. He felt lost and depressed over being helpless and alone. Was someone looking for him?

Dr. Rasper, checked Sage's pulse, temperature and blood pressure and recorded his findings. He looked over all the grafts and probed Sage's neck for pulses and his grafts for infection. All looked good. He stepped aside for Dr. Blaine to do his own probing.

Sage moaned as Dr. Blaine touched some sensitive areas. The pain medication was slowly wearing off. He moaned again which sounded more like a grunt and puff as he tried to get comfortable under the doctor's touch. The doctor called for the nurse and she returned with another injection of morphine to calm the patient down. She smiled at Sage again and lightly touched his brow as he slowly closed his eyes.

His last thought before he went into a deep sleep was, what a lovely smile the plain nurse had.

CHAPTER NINETEEN

Dr. Rasper looked over Sage's chart and noted the New York Police wanted to be informed as soon as the patient regained consciousness. He wanted to help the police find out who this man was too but he had to think of his patient first. This patient was traumatized and needed to rest more before having to relive this horrendous experience.

He made a note in the file to call a psychiatrist and a speech therapist to evaluate this John Doe. He moved onto his other patient files and forgot all about Sage.

***

Captain Kendall perused Sage's file once again and looked over the forensic pathologist's findings. Why didn't they find anything to connect Sage to these crimes? He had to be the one to commit them. *Where the hell was he now?* He couldn't have dropped off the face of the earth.

He called his two best officers together and gave them orders to check out John Doe at the hospital who was injured in the bear attack.

"Find out if this patient has regained consciousness and if the doctors know who he is. Ask to speak to the patient if he is conscious and report back to me. I will have a DNA sample taken from the patient to compare to Sage's mother when we can obtain hers. She is presently in a psychiatric hospital but not Dr. Fontana's. You will return the sample to me ASAP."

The two officers stood stiff and solemn as they answered, saluting their captain, "Yes, Sir!" They abruptly turned and quickly headed to their squad car.

"Looks like Cap is going crazy over this guy. Where do you think he's hiding? Do you think this John Doe is the same guy?"

"Who knows? But we may get lucky and talk to him. Maybe he can tell us if he saw Sage in the woods. Or better yet, the DNA sample may prove positive he is one and the same man."

"Poor guy is in a bad way by the sounds of his injuries on the report."

"Yeah, it might not be too pretty to see him. How's your stomach?"

"Not too good. How about yours?"

"Well, I didn't eat too much this morning, lucky for me. Otherwise, I might be wearing it."

"Oh, thanks for the description!"

***

Professor Jonas packed up her books and put her desk in order before leaving her classroom. She turned off the light and hefted her pocketbook to her left shoulder while balancing her heavy book bag onto her right. She turned and walked out to her car in the parking lot. She usually parked her car quite a distance away in order to put in some extra steps on her tracker.

She thought over how much she was enjoying her classes, especially the transfer from Professor Gyropolos' class, Mariah Hampton. She was quite intelligent and a quick learner. Mariah's last assignment had earned her an A plus which was unusual. Professor Jonas had rarely given that grade to any student in the past.

With her mind preoccupied the professor hadn't noticed the car sitting a few spaces away from hers and its occupant who was closely studying her every move.

***

Mariah was back at her apartment nursing her aching feet after a five-mile run. She had begun running, even though she wasn't good at it, in order to lose some weight. Being a student she had a tendency to sit too long studying and eat the wrong things at the café. She was trying to eat more salads instead of the delicious subs Tony always enjoyed. He had a high metabolism unlike hers.

She couldn't believe she was twenty. She was legally able to vote and make all decisions on her own. She had been making decisions on her own for a while though. She had grown up fast with all the problems and trauma she had had to deal with.

Mariah moved her mind away from her past and thought about her favorite professor. Professor Jonas was a joy to have as an instructor. Mariah had been in Professor Jonas' class now for a full semester and she signed up for the following semester to take her next class, Creative Writing.

Mariah was extremely proud of her latest grade – A plus. It was unheard of, so her classmates told her. "Jonas wouldn't give more than an A minus to anyone. She likes to keep her students on their toes."

Mariah knew she worked her butt off to complete the project and felt she earned the A plus. But she wouldn't say that to anyone. It would make her sound conceited.

She turned her attention back to her studies. She had much more to do for her other classes. Her grades were good but not as good as she knew she could do. She expected to have straight A's. In fact, she needed to have straight A's to stay in the advanced classes of the accelerated program to complete her degree. She would have to buckle down to get those B pluses up to A's and fast. Mariah looked up as the door opened.

Tony walked in and announced, "I'm home, my love. It's Friday! Let's go out to dinner somewhere. You have been straight out studying. You need to take off some time for fun and relaxation." Tony swept Mariah out of the chair and swung her around smothering her with kisses.

"Oh Tony, you are crazy! Stop before you make me sick to my stomach!" Mariah laughed uncontrollably as she held her stomach.

"Come on, let's go out to that nice Italian place with the checkered tablecloths. You mentioned you wanted to try it some time." Tony winked and puckered up as he placed Mariah back onto the chair again.

"You are one nutty guy, but I love you!" Mariah chuckled enjoying all this attention. "You know, you're right. I have been studying way too much lately. Let's get changed and go out. I would love some Italian food. I have been eating yogurt and salad all day. I need some carbs! Her new diet forgotten quickly."

"Okay, my lady, I'll jump in the shower and you can join me if you dare!" Tony gave Mariah his most beguiling smile.

"Ha, you funny man! I already took my shower. I will change and meet you in the kitchen in half an hour. Don't keep me waiting! I'm starving!" Mariah felt light and happy as she watched Tony walk away. He was so handsome. Those blue eyes of his still made her heart pitter patter along with his dark wavy hair.

***

Professor Jonas opened her eyes and looked around. The room was dark and damp. She ran her hands across the floor under her. Her fingertips were covered with grains of sand and dirt. Her head ached as she touched it gingerly. Her hand came away sticky. She was confused and disoriented. She tried to clear her mind as she thought back to the last thing she could remember. She was on her way to her car and juggling her book bag and pocketbook to get to her keys to open her car door. Then everything went black. How long had she been here? The only windows in the place were high above her head and there was no light coming it. It must still be night.

Where was she? She tried to move but found her ankle was chained to the wall behind her. She pulled the chain to see how much room she had to move but it came up short and she was yanked back painfully. Her ankle now throbbed from the pressure of the metal that dug into her tender skin.

She still had on her clothes but her jacket was missing and so were her bags. She felt her pockets for her cell. She had a habit of putting her cell into her back pocket of her pants in case she needed it in a hurry. She sighed in relief. It was still there. She pulled it out and tried to make a call. Cell service was poor but she kept moving the phone around her and up and down until she got a signal. She pumped in 911 and waited.

***

He had been watching her closely and waited in his car close to hers for his chance. She was fumbling with her keys trying to open her door. Now was his chance.

He rushed up behind her and knocked her over the head with a short metal rod he had tucked into the pocket of his coat. One swift hit and she was out.

He dragged her and her bags to his car and threw her and her belongings in. He was too much of a hurry to notice her keys had slid under her car.

He had the perfect place to keep her until he decided what to do next. His house had an unfinished dirt cellar which would suffice.

He drove slowly to his house to give his guest a place to stay. He chuckled to himself as he arrived and pulled her out of the car and tucked her bags into the trunk. He dragged her down to the cellar and chained her right ankle to the wall. He gave it a yank to make sure it was secure and left her, locking the door behind him.

She would be out for at least another half hour or so. He would have to inject her with one of his meds to keep her out until tomorrow. He didn't want to deal with her yet.

He would prepare some dinner and bring her his leftovers if he didn't finish it all. He laughed again at his own humor. He was a serious man unless some outlandish thing like this tickled his fancy.

He did his best to finish up his meal but, alas, there were a few fries and a slice of beef with gravy for his guest. He would bring her a bottle of water and a bucket to relieve herself.

***

She could hear someone coming down a set of stairs and a key in the lock. She sat up as quickly as she could to prepare to defend herself. She put away her cell. It had died, unfortunately, before she could say more than "help" to the operator.

The door opened and a light shone into her face blinding her temporarily. She blinked and tried to cover her face but at the same time wanted to know who her kidnapper was.

She heard his voice first. "Well, how are you doing, Professor Jonas? Do you like your new accommodations?" He mocked.

She gasped, "Professor Gyropolos! Why are you doing this to me? Where am I? You must let me go!"

"Oh, not so fast, my lady. All in due time. We have something to talk about first." Professor Gyropolos looked closely at his prisoner.

"Let me go now! Are you crazy?"

"Ha, I'm as sane as you are, Ellie! Isn't that your given name?"

"How do you know my name? I don't even know you well enough to know your first name?"

"Oh, I have ways of finding out. Now, let's discuss our lovely student, Mariah. It seems she has changed classes and is now in your Journalism class for this semester. If you want to leave here you have to do one thing for me."

"I don't care what you want. Let me out of here! You will regret ever doing this to me!" Ellie tried to sound strong and confident but was frightened out of her mind over this precarious situation.

"Okay, if that is the way you want it. I had brought you a delicious dinner and a water and of course a bucket for your toilet." He threw the dinner at her feet along with the bottle of water and bucket and turned to leave.

Ellie panicked and spoke up loudly, "Wait, please wait a minute. Don't leave me here. What do you want?" She watched his face in the dim light of the doorway. She could see him hesitate as he turned and came back.

"I see you have come to your senses. That's a smart thing to do, Ellie. Now let me begin again. What I need for you to do is talk to Mariah and tell her she cannot be in your class and must transfer back to mine."

"What? Why? What harm does it do for her to be in my class? She is doing well. She's my best student and a pleasure to have in class."

"Hmm, yes, I agree. That is why I want her back. She makes my class a pleasure to go to every week. I miss her lovely face."

"But there is no reason for me to do that."

"Oh, but there is, my dear. You either do this or I will kill you. Is this reason enough? In fact, not only are you going to do this but you are going to ask for a transfer to another college yourself as soon as possible. I want you out of here altogether."

"That doesn't make any sense. Why is it so important she be in your class?"

184

"You don't get to ask that question! I want her there! That's all you need to know!" He screamed at Ellie as he leaned into her face.

Ellie backed up away from his scarlet face as spittle hit her. She knew Professor Gyropolos was clearly out of his mind, and she feared for her life. She felt he would not let her go no matter what she did. Her only hope was to pray someone heard her say "help" on the phone before it died. Would they be able to find her?

She screamed as Professor Gyropolos grabbed her and injected a needle into her neck.

CHAPTER TWENTY

Mariah picked up her glass of Chianti and clinked glasses with Tony. She patted her full belly and smiled. "This was a wonderful meal and such a good idea, Tony. Thank you, honey."

"Ah, so you finally realized I had a good idea? Ha! I'm glad I convinced you to go out. I love this place! I want us to come here at least once a week from now on. I can't believe I ate all the chicken cutlet and pasta! I licked up all the sauce too. I have to compliment the chef."

"Yes, you did and you also finished up my veal cutlet and spaghetti. I can't believe you ate so much! Where do you put it?"

"I put it wherever it wants to go. I feel a five-mile run coming in my near future though."

Mariah suddenly appeared solemn and distracted. She looked up from staring into her wine and asked, "Tony, did you find out anything about Professor Gyropolos?"

"What do you mean, Mariah?"

"Well, I know you have been hanging around the office. Lexie, the secretary, told me. I talked to her for a long time recently when I stopped by to check on another class I have that was cancelled. She told me you were there shortly before I came in. I asked her what you were doing there."

"What did she tell you? Why would she tell you anything? Does she know we are an item?"

"Tony, everyone on campus knows we are an item. We live together for goodness sake!"

"Oh, yeah, okay. But what did she say?"

"Well, evidently you have been asking a lot of questions about the professor. She likes to talk and gave me some of the same information about him that she gave you. It appears he has been at other universities and had left suddenly. He is a creepy dude and keeps much to himself. He has a temper and gets a little weird at times when things don't go his way. She told me he got extremely upset about my transfer to Professor Jonas' class."

"Yes, she told me all this too. But you understand I need to know about this guy so I can protect you. He shouldn't be so interested in you like this. He is old enough to be your father." Tony was getting upset as he took another long sip of his wine to calm himself.

"It's okay. I understand how protective you are. I appreciate it too, really I do, Tony. But I don't want you to get too overprotective of me. I can take care of myself. I am being proactive. For instance, I bought a siren and a blinding light to attach to my keychain for protection. I will be ready for anything."

"Well, that's great, Mariah. That makes me feel better."

"I heard the sarcasm in your remark, Tony!"

"Sorry, but you need to keep them handy at all times when you are at school and traveling to and from classes. Please don't walk alone though. If you find you are alone call me and I'll be there to escort you wherever you need to go."

"See, there you go again! I'll be fine, Tony. Please don't worry so much. We don't even know where Sage is now."

Tony nodded but he wasn't thinking of Sage. He was more worried about a bizarre professor but didn't say this to Mariah. She was still going on and on about his overprotective nature.

The bill was placed on the table and Tony took care of it as he smiled at Mariah. She looked so lovely with her lustrous long brown hair and sparkling green eyes sitting there talking away about him. He knew he would do anything to protect her as he had done in the past.

***

"Phil, can you cover my phone calls? I need to check with the administrator about an odd call."

Kate dialed her supervisor and heard her voice immediately.

"What's wrong, Kate?"

"A couple of minutes ago I received a call and heard a woman's voice saying 'help' then it cut off but I did get a signal where it came from before it was lost."

"I sent some help her way but I wanted to let you know in case it's a bogus call."

"Good, we need to be sure. I will cover you if the police yell this way. You know I have your back and the backs of all my people. This job is not the easiest job. Don't worry, get back to work, okay?"

"Thanks."

"It's Maggie, Kate, you know that. No formality here unless you are in trouble," Maggie chuckled. In her position she had plenty of tension to go around and needed to keep her staff comfortable and alert. She was a tough boss when she had to be but she knew Kate was one of her best 911 operators.

Maggie looked over her staff from her window above the 911 center. She kept scanning her staff to ensure that they were alert and not having any difficulties. She would race down there to handle anything that came her way. Each call could save a life.

***

The police car drove up to the warehouse and parked. The two policemen skirted the building looking for a door to enter quickly. They had to go around the back before they found one.

They entered and turned on their flashlights when they couldn't find a light switch. They called out, "Is anyone here? This is the police. We received a call. Anyone hurt and need assistance?"

They waited but no sound could be heard. They moved through the warehouse and took the stairs to the basement. This room was darker and colder than upstairs. They surveyed the area without any sign of inhabitants.

Using their mikes they called into the station and reported there was no one in this place who could have called for assistance. They headed back to their car when they suddenly heard a scream.

"Did you hear that?"

"Yeah, where was it coming from?"

"Sounds like it came from the house next door. Let's check it out. The operator could have gotten the wrong coordinates. It could be there."

***

Mariah had two classes on Saturday and planned to stop by and see Professor Jonas afterward. She wanted to pass some ideas by her about her latest paper. She always enjoyed chatting and sharing her thoughts with the professor. Mariah had mentioned she might stop by after her classes and Professor Jonas had mentioned it was okay.

Mariah grabbed her bag and headed over to Professor Jonas' room. Upon reaching it she noticed a sign on the door, "Classes cancelled today."

That's bizarre, she thought. I wonder if Professor Jonas is sick. She appeared to be fine yesterday. Something wasn't right.

Mariah went in the direction of the office to find out more about why Professor Jonas had cancelled her classes. She knew it was none of her business but she had mentioned to the professor that she wanted to speak with her. *Maybe she left me a message.*

Mariah waited in line at the office for her turn to speak to Lexie, in the main office. It appeared everyone had a question for poor Lexie today. She checked her watch and decided to come back later to find out about Professor Jonas. After all, the professor probably had an unexpected appointment and had to cancel suddenly. Mariah figured she would come back after lunch and bring Lexie a coffee. She certainly looked like she needed one.

***

The police knocked on the door of the house and called out, "This is the police, open up."

Professor Gyropolos rushed upstairs and straightened out his clothes and smoothed back his hair as he prepared to open the door.

"Yes, officers. What can I do for you?"

"We heard a scream coming from this direction. Is everything all right?"

"Oh, yes officers, everything is fine. It was only my television. I'm sorry I must have had it on too loud. I shut if off when I heard your voice."

The officers exchanged glances after observing the weird look on the man's face as his eyes darted back and forth. He looked confused, disoriented, and anxious as if he was hiding something.

"Are you all right, sir?" One officer asked. The two officers had been trained to observe and decipher body language.

"Oh certainly, officer. I'm fine, perfectly fine." Professor Gyropolos tried to appear calm but he felt his heart thumping loudly in his ears.

Seeing the agitated demeanor and sweat beading up on the man's upper lip made the second officer request, "Sir, step aside. We need to come in and check out the premises to ensure you are safe and no one is in need of help."

The professor had no other alternative but to step aside and allow entrance to the policemen.

They entered the living room and looked around. Professor Gyropolos followed a distance between them from room to room. When they reached the kitchen and noticed the door to the cellar they stopped. They turned to look at the professor who looked even more anxious as they reached forward and turned the handle. They didn't notice the professor grab a large knife out of the kitchen drawer and hide it inside his jacket.

"After you, sir," the policemen announced to the professor as they followed him downstairs.

***

Mariah finished up her lunch and went back to the office with a cup of coffee in hand for Lexie. The line had dwindled down to two ahead of her. She caught Lexie's eye and held up the coffee.

Lexie smiled and nodded her thanks as she finished up with the last two students in the line.

"Hi Mariah. It's nice to see a happy face for a change. Everyone seems to be disgruntled today about something."

Mariah leaned over Lexie's desk and handed her the coffee. "Hope it's still hot. I rushed over as quickly as I could."

"Oh, don't worry I'll drink it anyway for the caffeine. Thank you so much, Mariah, for your thoughtfulness. I really need this. It's been crazy here. Haven't even stopped to have lunch yet," Lexie sighed as she took a large sip of coffee and smiled.

"What can I do for you, Mariah?" Lexie asked as she popped a cracker with cheese into her mouth and took another sip of coffee.

"Sorry about my eating. I'm starved."

"Please eat away. I understand fully. I can't think straight when I'm hungry," Mariah chuckled and continued, "Well, I was wondering why Professor Jonas cancelled her classes today. I had a meeting scheduled with her after her last class."

"Oh, yes, funny thing. She never showed up today for her classes. I tried calling her at home but no answer. It's not like her to do that – not call to tell us she wasn't coming in. She's one of the nicest instructors we have here. Always so pleasant and smiling and especially nice to me. Most professors nod in greeting but she stops by to chat. I'm worried, Mariah. Something isn't right. Her car was spotted in the parking lot too. That's peculiar because she is nowhere on campus."

"Her car is still here? That could mean she didn't leave or someone picked her up. Maybe she had car trouble." Mariah's mind began whirling with many possibilities.

"What do you think happened, Mariah? You look puzzled."

"I don't know but I don't like it either. What kind of car does she have?"

"It's a blue Ford Escape. She parks it in the last row near the walkway so she can get extra steps in. She told me that recently."

"Okay, thanks. Listen, I've got to go. If you hear from her let me know. Here's my cell. Talk to you later, Lexie."

Lexie called after Mariah, "Thanks again for the coffee."

Mariah raced back to her apartment to talk to Tony. She knew he would be there doing some work until she got home.

As she opened the door she called out, "Tony, honey, I need to talk to you. It's important."

"I'm in the office. Be right there."

"What's up, Mariah? Something happened? Did the professor bother you today?"

"Oh no, haven't seen him in a while. It's Professor Jonas. Something may have happened to her."

"Okay, sit down and explain. Do you need a cup of tea or anything stronger?"

"No, please listen, Tony." Mariah explained her concern for Professor Jonas' absence and reiterated what Lexie had told her about the Professor's car.

"Mariah, I think you may be worrying for nothing. Let me check it out. I'll ask around and see if anyone saw her when she left. I'll check out her car too. Maybe it broke down and she got a ride home."

"But then why didn't she come in today? She knew that I was going to meet with her after her last class. I feel something is wrong especially since she didn't call."

"Okay, okay, Mariah. Let me handle it from here."

"Thanks, Tony. You are one of a kind. I can always depend on you."

"Yeah, that's me – one of a kind! I'll do my best. Now let's relax. I can order a pizza, Chinese or tacos. What's your choice, my love?"

"I don't know, Tony. You pick. I'm not that hungry anyway."

"Oh, come on, honey. You got to eat. I'll get Chinese. I know you like that."

"Sure, that's fine."

"What? What do you mean fine? Honey, sit down and relax. I'll pour you a glass of wine. You can't take on everyone's problems. I bet Professor Jonas will be back to work on Monday. She probably needed a day off."

"Maybe, but please check it out all the same. Okay? I'd feel much better knowing she is okay."

"Yeah, I told you I would. Now, let's order and eat and relax. I have plans for you later." Tony gave Mariah his most beguiling smile.

"What plans?" Mariah chuckled.

***

Tony waited for Mariah to be asleep before he slipped out of bed and dressed. He wanted to check out Professor Jonas' car first then go to her house.

He drove over to the college and parked next to the blue Ford Escape. He turned on his flashlight as he inspected the car. He began by looking the car over from front to back. Next he shined the light under the car to inspect for leaks. He bent down to get a closer look when he saw a shiny object.

CHAPTER TWENTY-ONE

Sage had finally calmed down by the time the police arrived to speak with him. The police met with the doctor on call first and were led to the patient's room.

Sage watched as the two policemen entered his room. He was curious as to why they were there. It certainly wasn't to arrest a bear for attacking him. He poked fun at the thought. He didn't realize that he had a sense of humor, though a sick one. He hadn't figured out who he was yet.

The doctor introduced the patient to the police and left the room so they could talk to him. He waited outside the door in case he was needed to calm the patient down again.

"Sir, we're here to speak to you about what happened to you. Do you remember anything?"

Sage tried to speak but couldn't get the words out. He shook his head and moved his lips and mouthed the words in a raspy whisper, "No, I...I don't re...member any...thing." He coughed and choked as the words hurt his throat which was sore and would continue to be that way for a long time until it healed.

"We are looking for a man. Did you see anyone while you were in the woods?"

"No, I...I told you... I don't re...member any...thing." Sage gritted his teeth as the pain returned from his movements and his speech.

He pressed the call button and waited for the nurse to come back with his medication. He closed his eyes and ignored the police who continued to look at him.

"Well, if there is nothing you can tell us about seeing a man while you were in the woods, then I guess we will leave you. Sorry to disturb you. But if you do remember seeing anyone, please call. I'll leave a card here for you."

Sage opened his eyes and looked at the police, didn't answer, but nodded.

The nurse came in and administered the patient's medication as the police left the room. The nurse patted the patient on the arm. "Are you okay? The meds should kick in soon. Now relax and try to sleep. The police have gone. What did they want from you?"

Sage coughed as he whispered, "I don't…know. I don't re…member anything," Sage sighed and felt emotional as the nurse with the lovely smile studied him.

"It's okay. Don't push it. You don't have to talk. I know how difficult it must be for you. Just relax and try to sleep. You will feel better later. Here is a sip of water to bath your sore throat."

Sage nodded his thanks and closed his eyes.

***

"That was a rough thing to do, huh? He looked like he was in quite a bit of pain. Did you get a load of his face? His legs didn't look much better. He looked like a mean version of a Frankenstein."

"I know, don't remind me. I was getting hungry and I don't want to ruin my appetite thinking of how horrible he looked."

"I think we should call the Captain now instead of making him wait. It's a little drive back and I would like to stop for some lunch."

"No problem from me. I agree. I'll do the honors. You listened to his tirade last time."

"Captain, we saw the patient. He was in a bad way. He didn't even know who he was never mind if he saw anyone out there. He could hardly speak. I don't think we will get anything out of him. Doctor revealed he has a long road ahead of him. He may never recover his memory either."

"Okay, get yourselves back here. Take a few for lunch. I know you guys didn't get to eat. We'll talk more when you get here."

"Okay, Captain. Thanks. Will do."

"What did he have to say?"

"He wasn't happy but approved that we could stop for lunch and talk more about it when we get back. Hey, there's a diner up ahead. Let's stop there. I could use a burger. I wonder if they have good burgers there."

"I could eat a horse. Check the gas gauge too. We may be low. Captain will reimburse you if you pay for the gas, don't worry."

"Yeah, sure. I'm still waiting for the last time I did that."

"Well, either we fill up or we will be walking back part of the way."

"All right, all right. Let's do it so we can eat."

Saggy boobs brought over menus and placed them on the table for the police officers all the while snapping her gum and swishing her hips for their benefit.

"What can I get ya, officers? Do you want to hear the specials?"

"Um, sure." The policemen exchanged smirks as they took a gander at this older woman trying out her wiles on them. She leaned so far over the table to place napkins and utensils that her boobs brushed against their arms which they didn't get out of the way in time.

"We have chili, meatloaf, chicken pot pie and vegetable soup today."

"Do you need another minute to decide?"

"No, we both want burgers, fries and cokes."

"Okay, be ready in a jiffy. Are you on a case? We've had a lot of activity up this way since that guy got attacked. It should have been that guy who came here nearly a year ago. He was a mean dude with crazy eyes. I won't ever forget him. He gave me the creeps. I still have nightmares about him returning here."

The police looked up at her and asked, "What did you say?"

"Um, well, there was this strange guy who came here. I still get goosebumps when I think about him. I'm relieved he didn't come back. I thought he would to intimidate us like he did last time."

"What did he look like?"

The waitress explained what the man looked like, bald head, scruffy beard, crazy eyes and mean disposition. She then turned and went to get their lunch.

"Could it be him – Sage? He could have come this way. It was about that time when he disappeared. But then where did he go?"

"Your guess is as good as mine. He's probably long gone now. He could be out of state hunkering down until things cool down."

"Yeah, if he's smart he wouldn't come back here. Captain won't stop until he finds him."

After eating their burgers and fries, which they thought were surprisingly good for a greasy diner, they headed back to the precinct. They knew Captain Kendall would be interested in what the saggy boob waitress had to say.

***

Tony tried the keys in the lock and the door opened. He started the car and listened to the hum of the engine. Well, there was no problem with the car. But finding the keys on the ground did point to a few questions. How and why they got there. And where is their owner? He was beginning to agree with Mariah about strange things going on here. She may be right that something may have happened to Professor Jonas.

There was one thing he could do to find out. Look at the video from the camera overlooking the parking lot. He knew enough people on campus who could get the video feed for him without too many questions. He didn't want to cause any alarm yet.

Tony exited the car and turned to his own car to head back to the apartment. As he was about to open the car he heard a voice behind him.

"What did you find out, Tony?"

"Oh, Mariah, you gave me a start. What are you doing here?"

"I followed you. I knew you were up to some sleuthing. Now tell me what did you find? Was I right? Did something happen to the professor?"

"Well, you were right to worry. Something must have happened for she dropped her keys under her car as if she was in a hurry to open her door and was interrupted."

"Oh my God, Tony! What are we going to do? We need to find her?"

"I have a plan, honey. I'll get hold of the video from the parking lot cameras. There's bound to be some evidence there to tell us."

"Okay, let's go get them."

"Wait a minute, Mariah. It's late. No one's around now. But… I know one person who is still around, the custodian. He works nights. He might be able to help us get the video."

"Good idea, Tony! Come on, hurry up! Let's go find him."

"He has an office. He could be hanging out there now taking a breather. He doesn't work nonstop."

They went in the direction of the gymnasium where the custodial office was located. As they got closer they could hear a television.

Tony knocked loudly on the door to be heard over the television.

Ed Corbera jumped up from his nightly nap and shook his head to clear it. *Was that a knock on my door? Who the hell is it at this time of night? It better not be that creep of a boss checking up on me!*

Ed opened the door a crack and peered out at a man and woman staring back at him.

"Who are you and what do you want? You shouldn't be in the building at this time of night! How the hell did you get in?"

"Oh, sorry, but I do have a key. I am on staff as dean of students. My name is Tony Tremont and this is my girlfriend, Mariah Hampton. She's a student here."

"Okay, okay, enough with the introductions! I'm Ed. Nice to meet ya! Okay, now leave." Ed closed the door in Tony's and Mariah's faces and planned to go back to his nap. But, that wasn't to be.

Tony turned the knob and pushed the door open nearly knocking Ed off his feet.

"Hey, what do you think you're doing?"

"Listen, Ed, we have something to tell you and need your help."

Mariah gave Ed her brightest smile as he looked at both of them, clearly confused and not at all happy.

"What do you want?" Ed asked in a gruff, standoffish manner.

"Can we come in please?" Tony offered his own smile to put the custodian at ease.

"All right, come in," Ed answered reluctantly but didn't open the door wide enough for them to enter. They had to push it open more as they moved into the claustrophobic room which had only a small desk, chair and TV.

"Can you turn down the TV, Ed, so that we can talk?"

"Okay, let's get this over with. I have work to do."

Tony smirked knowing full well that Ed was only going to go back to sleep and work was nowhere on his mind.

"Listen, Ed," Tony explained all about the car, the missing professor, and his need to see the video of the parking lot.

"Now do you understand how important this is? Professor Jonas could be in serious trouble, harmed or maybe even…" Tony looked over at Mariah but didn't finish his thought. She knew what he was going to say, exchanged looks with him and cringed.

"Okay, come with me. It's in the video room. All the tapes are kept there for safety from dust and chemicals. I use lots of chemicals cleaning this place."

Tony sat at the desk and pulled up the latest video from the past 24 hours. He rewound it until he saw Professor Jonas arrive in her car. They all watched as she parked and came into work. They scanned it ahead until they saw her come back out to her car.

"Tony, look at that other car across from hers? Can you bring it in closer so we can see the driver's face?"

Tony focused on the driver and both of them took in a shocked breath.

"Oh no, it's Professor Gyropolos! He's watching her. Move it ahead quickly, Tony."

They watched and held their breaths as Professor Gyropolos got out of his car and came up behind Professor Jonas who was juggling her bags and trying to put the keys into the lock of her car door.

Mariah cried out as she watched Professor Gyropolos grab Professor Jonas and hit her over the head with a stick or pipe.

"Oh my God, why did he do that? He's dragging her to his car, Tony! We've got to find him!"

"Yes, I know, Mariah. We need his address. Try finding it online while I call the police."

Mariah went online to get the address. Her hands were shaking and it took her longer to calm them down in order to spell out his name.

Ed stood back and observed the two. "Well, it looks like your professor is in trouble. You should let the police take care of this. This guy looks to be dangerous. What would make him do that to a fellow staff member?"

"I don't know Ed. All I know is that we need to find him and then we will find Professor Jonas. He has to have her locked up somewhere. I agree with you about the police but sometimes they are not fast enough. We'll have to help them along."

Turning toward Mariah he grabbed her hand and ran out of the room saying, "Thanks, Ed, for your help."

"Yeah, sure whatever," Ed responded as he locked up the video room and headed back to his office.

Tony dialed the police and asked for the captain to report a crime.

The dispatcher patched Tony through when he explained what he had seen and who he was, a private investigator, at least he was previously.

"Captain Alvarez. Who is this?"

"Captain, I'm sorry to pull you away from other things but I think this is important. I'm Tony Tremont. I was involved in the Sage case."

"Ah, yes I remember you, Tony. I heard all about that from Captain Kendall in New York. I've been following this case. What can I do for you?"

Tony explained about the kidnapping of the Professor and what he saw on the video and waited for the Captain to respond.

"I see, Tony. I trust your judgment. I'll send out some men to check the tapes and confiscate them for evidence. In the meantime we will obtain Professor Gyropolos' address and send out a couple of officers to check out his residence for this Professor Jonas."

Mariah chirped up with the professor's address as Tony was listening to the Captain.

"Oh Captain, here's the address." He spouted off the address from Mariah's phone and thanked the captain and then hung up.

"Well, what did he say, Tony? Did he believe you? What is he going to do?"

"Of course he believed me. He knows me from previously when we captured Sage. He indicated that he would follow-up and get the tapes for evidence and send two men to Professor Gyropolos' residence to check it out."

***

Back at Professor Gyropolos' cellar he was busy burying the two officers in a separate part of the dirt cellar away from Professor Jonas. He wiped the sweat and blood from his brow with his handkerchief from stabbing the two officers as he continued to dig a large enough hole to bury the men. He pulled off his coat and buried it too because if was soaked with the officer's blood.

When he had stabbed the first officer the second had turned and pulled out his gun. The gun went off but missed hitting Professor Gyropolos because the professor had swung his knife at the officer and knocked the gun away.

Professor Jonas was still out and unaware of what was taking place across from her present surroundings.

CHAPTER TWENTY-TWO

Sage was feeling more alert but still in pain now that the morphine was wearing off. He was hooked up to a pump which he could now administer as needed. He pressed the pump and sighed. He looked around the room for the nurse. She had left. He liked looking at her sparkling blue eyes and lovely smile. She wasn't a beautiful woman but there was something special about her in her eyes. He thought it over and decided it was her kindness toward him. He couldn't remember if anyone had ever been kind to him like that.

She had refused that morning to give him a mirror so he could see what he looked like now. He knew his injuries were severe and he would never look like he did previously, whatever that was. She didn't appear to be frightened though or turned off by his looks. So it couldn't be too bad, he thought, or could it?

As he continued to muse about his appearance, his favorite nurse appeared by his side with his medications. He wanted to wean himself off of the morphine and get out of this hospital but he didn't know where he would go. He didn't know where he lived. Maybe the nurse would help him.

"How's my favorite patient doing today?"

"Oh, I'm …doing better… I think." Sage looked at those kindly eyes and actually tried to smile but something was wrong he couldn't feel his lips or cheeks responding.

"You are sounding better. Your voice is getting stronger. The Speech Therapist has done a good job with you."

Sage nodded and grimaced.

"It's okay. Your facial muscles need to learn how to react again. They have been damaged but you will adjust and learn how to smile again. It will be a different and unique smile, that's all. But all smiles are beautiful." The nurse smiled at Sage as she checked the pump for his medication and adjusted his sheets, pillows, and blankets to make him more comfortable.

"What's…your…name?" Sage was shocked that he actually asked that question but waited anxiously for her response.

"Arabella. My mother named me after my grandmother. It's an old-fashioned name, I know. But most people call me Ara or Bella."

"Arabella, I...like...it." Sage tried out his smile once again.

"There you go. Your smile is getting wider and more beautiful all the time. What do you want me to call you? The police and hospital call you John Doe. It's too common and you are anything but common."

"What...would...you...like to...call...me?"

"Hmm, let's see. I would like to give you an old-fashioned name to go with mine. I think you look like a Sherman. What do you think about that name?"

"Sher...man? Okay, I guess...if you...like...it. I will...be...Sherman. Sound...good."

"Good, that's wonderful, Sherman. Now we need to give you a last name. Do you have any preferences?"

"No, not...really. Something...that goes...with Sherman."

"Yes, I agree. Let's see, how about Wallace? That was my grandmother's maiden name."

"Sherman   Wallace.   That…is…perfect. Thank…you…Arabella."

Arabella, smiled and her eyes twinkled as she admired her beloved patient. She only wished she knew who he was. She was beginning to have feelings for him. His scars did not scare her for she had been a nurse long enough to have seen worse. It was what was inside the person that mattered, and Sherman Wallace had a good heart. She was sure of it.

Sherman Wallace observed Arabella as she smiled so beautifully. Suddenly he got a sharp pain in his head and a flash of something horrible passed through – an old woman and a dog covered in blood. He cringed and shook his head to erase it. *What was that? Did I do that?*

Arabella stopped talking and looked at Sherman. "What's the matter, Sherm? Are you in pain?"

"No,   I'm…okay.   I   got…pain   in   my head…saw…things. It's…nothing. I'm…fine."

Arabella looked at Sherman's vitals and noticed his blood pressure was elevated. "I'll be right back with the doctor. I want him to check you over. Rest for now."

"Arabella, I'm...fine. Don't...leave." Sherman closed his eyes and tried to erase what he had seen. He could never do that to anyone, especially an old woman and a dog.

The ebony doctor, (Dr. Rasper) returned and took Sherman's pulse, BP, and temperature and reviewed his chart. He looked over all the skin grafts and nodded to himself. All looked exceptional. The patient was doing exceedingly well since he had awoken from his coma. His body defenses were responding remarkably fast.

"Doctor, is the patient all right?" Arabella whispered as she accompanied Dr. Rasper out of the room.

"Oh, he is doing exceptionally well. It's surprising that he has come along so quickly. I think you may be responsible for this sudden recovery. He will be ready to leave within the next couple of weeks."

"Thank you, Doctor, but what did I do that I don't already do for all the patients?"

"Oh, I think he has taken a liking to you and you to him. You do seem to spend a lot of time here before, during, and after the other patients." Dr. Rasper smiled and patted her on the arm as he left to continue his rounds.

"Oh, my, I guess I do." Arabella found herself blushing. She rushed back to Sherman to tell him the good news.

Sherman opened his eyes when he heard Arabella's voice. She was smiling and looking pleased.

"Well, Sherman, I have some extremely good news to share with you."

"I'm…not…going to…die?"

"Oh dear, no. You are not going to die, Sherman. Doc reported that you will be able to leave the hospital and go home in two weeks. You are doing exceptionally well."

"Really? But…where…will…I go? I don't…know…where I…live." Sherman hung his head and closed his eyes tightly to keep the tears from falling. He was frightened about leaving. He didn't know where he would go.

"Well," Arabella mused and tapped her fingers on the side of the bed rail. "You can come home with me. I have a large Victorian that was my grandmother's and there are plenty of rooms. It's only my mother, me and my cat, Geronimo. I'll help you, Sherman. Your memory could come back any time, the doctors indicated." Arabella whispered under her breath...*or hopefully never.*

"But...I can't...pay...you, Arabella. I can't...take advantage of your...kindness. I will find...somewhere to go. Don't...worry...about...me."

"No, I insist, Sherman. You're going to stay with me. I won't take 'no' for an answer. Now, rest until lunch. I have other patients to see. I'll stop by after lunch."

"Arabella, thank you. I don't...know how...I will...ever repay you." Sherman sighed. His throat was aching from trying to talk. Arabella had left a cup of ice water on his tray. He took a gulp and rested his head back on his pillow.

"Don't think about it now, Sherman. Everything will work out for the best. Don't worry." Arabella left Sherman with her glorious smile and sparkling, azure blue eyes.

Sherman closed his eyes and sighed. She was one special person in his life. He wondered if there were others. *Do I have a wife and children? Siblings? Parents? Will they be looking for me?*

He would try to make a new life for himself. Stay with Arabella and get stronger and then find a job so he could repay her for her kindness. Then he would move on. But did he want to leave Arabella? He was beginning to have some feelings for her.

Sherman drifted off to sleep and a flash of memory once again attacked him even more viciously this time.

He screamed out when he saw himself cutting the neck of an old woman and kicking a dog in the head. He watched in slow motion as the woman's eyes bugged out of her head in shock and the blood spurted out of her neck all over him. He saw the dog's limp body and his neck at an odd angle.

Sherman thrashed and kicked trying to get away from this dream or memory or whatever it was.

Dr. Rasper raced into Sherman's room when he heard the patient's screams.

"Wake up! You're having a bad dream. It's okay, you are safe here."

Sherman opened his eyes and looked at the doctor.

"Was I dreaming…or was it…real?"

"Oh, it was only a dream. You went through a horrendous experience. It is not unusual to have nightmares for a while. They will fade in time as your mind heals too."

"But I…" Sherman stopped himself. He had not been dreaming of the bear attack. He didn't even remember the bear attack yet. All he could see in his mind was an old woman and a dog dying. *Did he do that? How could he do that? Would more horrible memories soon surface? What kind of person was he?*

Arabella was out of breath as she came into Sherman's room. The doctor was leaving and she stopped him and asked, "What happened to Sherman? Is he okay?"

"Sherman, who's Sherman?" The doctor looked at her with a bewildered expression.

"Oh, I gave him a name. I didn't want to keep calling him 'hey you' or 'John Doe.'"

"Oh, I see." But the doctor really didn't and continued to walk away.

Arabella reached out to grab his arm, "No Doctor, don't leave. Please tell me about the patient. Is he all right?"

"Yes, Arabella, he is going to be fine. His memory is kicking in. With the horrendous experience from the bear attack, he is bound to have nightmares. No need to worry. We can give him a tranquilizer to help him relax. I want to wean him off the morphine. He appears to be agitated and needs to rest. I'll have a psychiatrist do a consult on him."

"Okay, thank you, Doctor."

"I will put it in his chart what to give him. Check at the desk. Tonight he will have his first dose."

"All right, Doctor. I'll check at the desk after I see him."

Dr. Rasper looked kindly at Arabella. "Listen, Arabella, you don't even know who this man really is. Be careful, don't move forward until you do know more about him."

"Oh, I think I know who he is without knowing his real name. I see him as a kind and lost soul. I will help him as much as I can."

"I know you will, Arabella. But be careful you may get hurt." The doctor silently thought, *you may be in more danger than you know.* He remembered the look of not only horror but anger on the patient's face. Who knows what he's hiding. There may be more than the bear attack in his memory.

CHAPTER TWENTY-THREE

Tony put Professor Gyropolos' address into his GPS and tried to keep his speed under control. He didn't want to be stopped by the police. That could delay or keep them from getting to the professor's house.

Mariah leaned forward and looked at the GPS and watched the houses flash by. She was anxious to get there too. But what would they do if they arrived before the police?

"Tony, what if the police aren't there yet? What can we do? We shouldn't confront him alone. He may be armed and dangerous."

"I agree, Mariah. I'm not going to put your life in danger. You're going to stay in the car while I go in. I won't go in unless the police are there already. Okay?"

"Well, okay, but I'm going in with you. Who will have your back? He can't get to both of us the same time especially if the police are there."

Tony slowed down as he saw the professor's house next to a large warehouse and a police car out in front of the warehouse.

"Well, that's strange."

"What, Tony? What's strange?"

"The police parked in front of the warehouse next door. Why didn't they park in front of the professor's house? Granted, it's not too far to walk but it doesn't make sense."

"I agree, that is weird. Well, let's go see what's happening. They must be checking out his place and have him in handcuffs by now. Hopefully they found Professor Jonas too."

"I hope so, Mariah. I truly hope so. Now stay behind me." Tony pulled out his revolver and held it in front of him as he pushed Mariah safely behind him.

"I'm fine, Tony. You don't have to keep pushing me back. I'm going to stay close to you."

Tony rolled his eyes but Mariah didn't see him do it. He knew how strong and stubborn Mariah could be. He didn't want to argue with her but would keep her behind him no matter what happened and he would shoot first if the professor tried anything.

They went up the stairs and knocked on the door. It was eerily quiet inside. Tony turned to Mariah. "That's odd. We should be hearing or seeing the police here. Where are they?"

"Maybe they're questioning him in another room away from the door. I'm sure they have things under control. I only pray that they have found Professor Jonas unharmed."

"Ssh, listen. Someone is coming to the door. I hear footsteps."

Professor Gyropolos stopped digging and smoothed out the dirt over the policemen and turned to go upstairs. He could hear knocking.

Who the hell is that now? Who knows where I live? It can't be more police.

As Professor Gyropolos opened the door to the kitchen he walked through the living room, looked out the window and saw two figures, a man holding a gun and Mariah. *What were they doing here? The man must be Mariah's boyfriend. This is perfect. Now I don't have to go to her. He bought her to me.*

Professor Gyropolos put on his best smile and opened the door. "Well, isn't this an unexpected surprise. It's lovely to see you both. How are you

Mariah? Please come in. This must be your boyfriend, Tony, is it?"

Tony hid his gun in his pocket, hesitated for a moment and tried to look over the professor's shoulder for the police. They were not in the living room or the kitchen. *Where were they?*

"Please come in. I'll put on some tea." He leered at Mariah and reached forward to pull them into his house.

Mariah pulled away from the professor's reach but too late. Tony lost his balance and fell into the living room losing his gun in the process with Mariah tumbling on top of him. Professor pulled them both into the house and shut the door, locking it behind him.

Before Tony could reach his gun, Professor Gyropolos picked it up and pointed it at him.

"Now what do you need this for, Tony? Were you expecting to shoot me? Why would you want to shoot a professor? You aren't even in my class. I can understand if you were and received a poor grade. Then you may want to shoot me." Professor Gyropolos laughed but the sound was not pleasant and did not reach his eyes, which appeared glazed.

Mariah kicked out at Professor's legs and tried to knock him down to protect Tony but only caused the gun to be directed toward her.

"Well, you are a feisty one, aren't you Mariah. No wonder your Uncle Sage enjoyed hunting you."

"What did you say? My Uncle Sage? How do you know him?" Mariah trembled hearing his name. *How did the Professor know Sage?*

Professor Gyropolos chuckled and appeared to be enjoying himself. He loved the shocked look on Mariah's lovely face. He particularly liked putting fear into his victims. These two would be fun to torment before he killed them. He would make sure to torture Mariah first then Tony will beg to be killed.

"Well, wouldn't you like to know, sweet Mariah? I have been observing and learning from your Uncle Sage from a distance. He is quite talented. Wouldn't you say? I only hope to emulate him and maybe improve his craft a little. There is always room for improvement. Don't you think so, Mariah?"

Tony leaned forward and looked Professor Gyropolos in the eyes. It wasn't pleasant because Tony could see how unstable this man really was.

He had to keep his cool and talk to the professor and convince him to let Mariah go.

"Let's go see a friend of yours. She will be thrilled to see you, Mariah. She is downstairs. Open the door, Tony, and slowly walk downstairs. Don't try anything funny. Remember, I have the gun now and it will be aimed at Mariah. One wrong move and she will be dead, you next. Let's not ruin this lovely time together. Tony, turn to your right and open that door. Oh, sorry, I have the key. Wait a minute please."

Professor Gyropolos pulled the key from his pocket and pushed Tony and Mariah aside never taking his eyes off of them as he unlocked the door.

It was darker in the room then outside and they had to let their eyes adjust to the dim interior. They could make out a lump next to the front wall of the dirt cellar. Was it Professor Jonas?

"Oh, Professor Jonas, you have company dear. Wake up, wake up, sleepy head."

Professor Gyropolos pushed Tony and Mariah farther into the room as he spoke to the lump. They walked over to it and looked closer.

Professor turned on his flashlight and directed the beam toward the lump.

Mariah cried out when she saw Professor Jonas's dirt-smeared face. She shook her shoulder. "Professor, are you all right? It's Mariah."

Professor Jonas moaned and turned toward the voice. "Oh, Mariah! What are you doing here? He has you too? You can't stay. You must get away. He's dangerous. He'll kill you too!"

"Ha, you are a smart one, Professor Jonas! But I will kill you first, my dear, then Mariah and finally Tony. Oh, have you met Tony, Professor? He's Mariah's beau. Isn't it sweet that he brought her all the way over here to be with me? He saved me much stress trying to get her here myself. Oh, this is such a lovely party we are going to have!"

Mariah locked eyes with Tony as her mind whirled with ideas about how they would all get away. She looked around her and noted there were only a couple of windows high above their heads. This room appeared to be completely dug out and the walls were in the process of being cemented. Professor Jonas coughed and shivered on the damp floor.

Mariah bent down and hugged her and whispered. "Are you okay? We're going to get you out of here, I promise. I don't know how yet but I'm working on it. Can you move your leg any farther from the wall?" Professor Jonas whispered, "No, I've tried so much that I rubbed my ankle raw. I will keep trying though. I think the chain is getting loose from the wall."

Mariah leaned in to take a look at the chain that was screwed into the dirt wall. It definitely was loose. While Tony kept Professor Gyropolos busy talking she dug around the screw and loosened it more and gave it a swift yank. It pulled free.

Mariah whispered into Professor Jonas' ear, "I pulled it away from the wall. Pretend that you are still restrained but work on getting it off your ankle. Here's a hair pin. Maybe that will fit into the hole and loosen the lock."

Tony kept Professor Gyropolos talking. "So Professor, what are your plans now that you have three of us here? I can't imagine you will need the ladies. Why don't you let the ladies go? You and I can have a nice chat. I may even share some of Sage's exploits with you if you let the women go."

"Hmm, that is very tempting, Tony. But I cannot do that. I didn't want you, just the ladies. I have such exciting plans for them. It will be a pleasure to have their company for a little longer. They are both beautiful women, don't you think, Tony? It would be a shame to ruin their faces. But, alas, I must continue with my plans to live up to Sage's standards."

"Professor, don't you wonder where Sage is right now? Do you want me to contact him so you can meet him?"

"Oh my, can you do that, Tony? I didn't know you even knew where he was. The police don't seem to know. How would you know?"

Tony could see the interest in the professor's eyes as he continued to distract him as the women worked on the chain attached to Professor Jonas' ankle. He looked over at Mariah and she shook her head – Professor Jonas' ankle was still attached.

"Well, I will tell you as soon as you let the women go. Sage keeps in touch with Mariah's family and so do I. He is closer than you think. He would be quite impressed to hear that you are following in his footsteps. But, Professor, you have a lot to learn yet.

And, you can learn it all from Sage, the master. What do you think?"

"Well, well, well, Tony, you are a scoundrel, aren't you? I know what you are doing. You are trying to distract me from the ladies."

Turning toward the women Professor Gyropolos asked, "Well, my lovelies. What are you two doing over there? You seem awfully cozy. Is everything copacetic?" He laughed in his creepy nasally way that put chills in everyone around him.

"We're fine, Professor. You have not taken care of Professor Jonas very well. She is chilled to the bone and I am trying to warm her up."

Mariah gave Professor Jonas a hug and whispered into her ear, "The chain is off your ankle. Try to keep still and wait for my signal to move."

Professor Jonas nodded and coughed again. Mariah met Tony's eyes and nodded slightly. He blinked back at her and moved closer to Professor Gyropolos who was paying more attention to the women then him. Professor Gyropolos looked back at Tony as he moved and directed the gun back to him.

"Now Tony, what do you think you were going to do? Attack me? Ha, do you think I can't stop you. I stopped two policemen who came here earlier and killed them. They are buried in the room across from this. I have room enough for all of you there." Professor Gyropolos announced with a smirk.

Tony looked over the professor's shoulder at Mariah and nodded. Mariah rammed into the back of the professor's legs and knocked him down. Tony joined in and wrestled the gun out of his hands as Professor Jonas hit Professor Gyropolos over the head, knocking him out with the thick end of the chain that had kept her prisoner. The three held Professor Gyropolos down, in case he wasn't completely out, until Tony could wrap the chain around the Professor's hands. They needed to leave the basement and wait upstairs for the police before Professor Gyropolos woke up.

***

Back at Vermont Police Station, Captain Alvarez was trying to contact the policemen who were supposed to report back to the precinct after following up on a 911 call. They had called in shortly after they arrived at the location and reported it was a false alarm.

"Where the hell are those men? I sent them out over two hours ago! They better not be at a coffee shop enjoying their coffees!"

***

Tony and Mariah pulled Professor Jonas along out of the room and up the stairs. As Tony opened the cellar door to the kitchen they heard knocking on the front door.

A quick look out the window in the living room revealed two policemen standing on the front porch looking clearly disgruntled. Tony pulled open the door and explained what had previously transpired and where to find the Professor and two dead policemen's bodies. One officer pulled out his mike and called Captain Alvarez to report what Tony had relayed.

"What the hell! He killed two of my men? I'll send an ambulance and the coroner. Is Professor Jonas all right? Send her in the ambulance so she can be checked out. I want you two to stay put and report everything you find ASAP. I will dispatch another car to help you out. Send Tony and Mariah to my office! Son of a bitch!" Captain kept on swearing as he finally hung up the phone. He quickly called his friend, Captain Kendall of New York, to report what was going on with this Sage imitator.

"Sounds like Captain Alvarez is a little upset." Tony sympathized with the officers. He has a reason to be. He certainly doesn't need another Sage!"

"Yeah, that's for sure. You and Mariah will need to go to the station to talk to Captain Alvarez—his orders. He wants to hear it directly from you. An ambulance is coming for you, Professor Jonas."

"Okay, Officers. No problem for us. We are happy to do that. It's been a harrowing experience. Glad it's all over." Tony pulled Mariah in for a hug and she, in turn, hugged Professor Jonas who was not looking well. She was still shivering. A short time later an ambulance pulled up and came in to get Professor Jonas. A coroner's wagon drove into the driveway as the ambulance left. Two more policemen arrived right behind and joined the group in the kitchen.

"Can we leave now, Officers?" Tony asked before the officers all disappeared down in the basement.

"Sure, go ahead."

Tony added, "Oh, be careful, Professor Gyropolos will probably be awake and try to give you a hard time. He is a sneaky SOB."

"Yeah, we've met his kind before. We've got it from here. Go directly to the station. Captain Alvarez is waiting for you. Do either of you need an ambulance?"

"No we're fine, a little shook up, is all. We'll recover, won't we, Mariah?" Mariah nodded and smiled, relief showing on her face.

"Yes, I'm okay," Mariah sighed and held onto Tony as they exited the house to his car.

CHAPTER TWENTY-FOUR

Sage woke up in a sweat as he continued to have more nightmares about killing people. He tried to sit up but was still connected to machines. He buzzed for the nurse and waited as he wiped his brow with his sheet.

Arabella rushed into the room surprised that she had been summoned by Sherman. "Are you okay, Sherm? What's wrong? I came as soon as I could."

"I...I had another bad dream, that's all. Can you give me a cool towel? I'm sweating. I need some water too."

"Of course, Sherman. I'll be right back." Arabella left his room and hurried back to the nurses' station to get a towel and a cup of water. She was concerned that Sherman was having these dreams. He didn't mention what they were about though. She would have to try to get him to open up to her. She didn't want to push too hard. Who knows what he had to tell her. For the first time she was frightened but didn't know why. He was such a sweet man. It had to be the bear attack. She couldn't imagine having to go through an event so traumatic and not be affected profoundly in some way.

Arabella leaned over Sherman and wiped his face gently and sat him up to drink his water. She announced, "The doctor will be in shortly to disconnect you from the heart monitor and release your straps so you can sit up on your own."

Other than the bad dreams, the patient was coming along well. He was being seen by a psychiatrist who reported on the patient's file that Sherman was doing as well as could be expected considering what he had gone through.

Arabella waited for Sherman to calm down to ask him about his dreams. "Are you okay now, Sherman? Can I ask you what you were dreaming about?" Arabella gave Sherman her widest smile that made her eyes sparkle.

Sherman looked kindly upon her face and shook his head. "I can't talk about it. I'm sorry, Arabella, I don't…want to talk…about it."

"That's okay. In time you will feel more comfortable about telling me. We will have plenty of time to do that. After all, you are staying with me in a couple of weeks, doctors' orders."

Sherman looked surprised at her words. "Does the doctor…know I'm staying…with you? Did he…order you…to do that?"

"That's two questions, Sherm. The first answer is 'yes' and the second is 'no.' I did that on my own. I wanted to help you and I thought you liked the idea of coming to my house."

"Oh…of course, I do, Arabella. I want…to go to your house. I don't…want to be…a burden. I will repay you for your…hospitality as soon as I…fully recover and get a job…or find out…who I am - whichever comes first." Sherman cringed to think about the second part of his statement. Would he be happy to know who he really was?

***

Tony and Mariah sat at the precinct and went over their statements again with Captain Alvarez and Captain Kendall on the speaker phone. Captain Alvarez was jotting down notes while a secretary recorded everything that was discussed.

Two policemen were on their way to the hospital to obtain Professor Jonas' statement as soon as she was cleared by the doctor.

Captain Kendall spoke. "Tony, I think you handled yourself well in these trying circumstances. If you ever want to become a cop, let me know. I could use you on my force. You wouldn't make mistakes like some of these men have done and lost their lives in the process. What happened to make two police officers lose their lives? What a waste!"

Captain Alvarez added, "These were some of my best men. They evidently made some blunder and grossly underestimated the perp."

"Sorry to interrupt your thoughts, Captain Alvarez and Captain Kendall, but this Professor Gyropolos is an unstable character. I never expected him to be so savvy. He's crazier than Sage and maybe more dangerous!"

Captain Kendall acknowledged, "Yes, I agree with you, Tony, and I haven't even met the guy. I'm looking forward to meeting him and finding out what makes him tick. It takes all kinds to make up our insane world. Now if we only could find Sage. I would be a happy man."

"Yes, I agree with you wholeheartedly, Captain Kendall. We want to see him behind bars for good."

Tony waited a moment to let the captains collect their thoughts. "Are we all through here, Captain Alvarez and Captain Kendall?"

Captain Kendall answered, "Oh, sorry? I was lost in my thoughts about Sage. I apologize for making you upset, Mariah. I know what you went through a year ago. This has been a trying time for you and must have opened up old wounds and memories. Do you need to go to the hospital?"

Mariah looked at Tony and sighed, "No, I'm okay now. I'm relieved that we found Professor Jonas alive. I would like to go visit her now. Thank you both, Captain Alvarez and Captain Kendall, for your concern. Oh, and congratulations on your promotion, Captain Alvarez."

"Thank you, Mariah. It's good to see you again. Sorry about these tragic circumstances."

"Yes, they seem to be following me, Captain."

Captain Alvarez shook both their hands. "Of course, please feel free to leave. If we need you again we'll call. Stay local for now, okay?"

"Yes, Captains, we will," Tony and Mariah replied together.

"Thank you both for what you did. You saved that woman's life. She has you to thank and not Lindan, Vermont's finest," Captain Alvarez added.

Tony nodded, guided Mariah out of the precinct and drove to the hospital to check on Professor Jonas. Mariah laid her head on the back of the seat and closed her eyes and sighed.

Tony patted her hands which were tightly held in her lap. "Mariah, maybe we should go home so you can rest. It has been a horrendous experience for you."

"Not only for me but for you and especially Professor Jonas. I want to see her and make sure she's okay. Then and only then will I be able to rest."

Tony assented. He knew when not to argue with Mariah. Tony smiled knowing that she was his, demanding or not.

***

By the time they arrived at the hospital fifteen minutes away from the police station, Mariah was asleep.

Tony gently touched her shoulder and whispered in her ear, "Mariah, we're at the hospital?"

Mariah opened her eyes and nodded. "Okay, I guess I must have fallen asleep. Sorry about that, Tony. Let's go see the professor. Then we can go home."

"Yes, good idea, Mariah." Tony smiled and let her lead the way to the lobby where she asked the receptionist where to find Professor Jonas.

"Do you have a first name for the patient?" The receptionist asked.

"Umm, sorry, no I don't. She must have arrived a short time ago. Maybe she's in the ER."

The receptionist dialed the ER and gave the patient's last name and waited.

"Yes, she's still there but will be going up to her room shortly on the third floor, room 305. Give her ten minutes to get settled there."

"Oh, thank you very much." Mariah turned to Tony and relayed the news. We can go up in ten minutes once she's settled. They will be keeping her overnight for observation."

"That's a good idea because she could have gotten pneumonia in that cellar lying on the damp dirt floor. I still don't understand why Professor Gyropolos would want to harm her. What did she do to him? It was me that he was angry with because I changed classes. But he talked about killing us both - over changing classes? He is one sick individual!"

"Well, Mariah, Professor Gyropolos did say he was trying to emulate Sage. He was certainly doing a good impression of Sage."

Mariah shivered at the thought of Sage and what could have happened to them if they hadn't gotten away from the professor. She shook her head and mused over having two crazy men in her life who wanted to kill her. What were the odds of this happening?

"A penny for your thoughts, Mariah? Are you okay?"

"Yeah, I'm fine. I was thinking over what could have happened to us if we hadn't escaped."

"Please don't think about it. It's over. Professor Gyropolos will be put away for kidnapping and murder. He won't be going anywhere for a long time."

"We can only hope, Tony. Remember Sage. He was hard to put away, and now is, only God knows where."

"Hmm, yes, but we will find Sage. He can't hide away forever. He needs to continue his killing streak and will come out of hiding soon. We will be ready for him."

"Oh, Tony, I plan to be ready for him. He will not get close enough to touch me. I'm going to get myself a gun and I will use it if necessary."

"Whoa, wait a minute, Mariah. I don't want to see you handling a gun. You don't even know how to use it."

"I will learn. There's a shooting range nearby."

"Okay, but I'm going with you. I could use some practice myself. Make an appointment and let me know when. I'll drive."

***

The receptionist motioned to Mariah that it was okay to go up to Professor Jonas' room now.

The Professor was sitting up in bed when they walked in. She was hooked up to saline and a blood pressure cuff but managed to look okay.

"Oh, Mariah and Tony, thank you for coming. I didn't expect you to come. You should be home resting yourselves. I can't thank you both enough for coming to my rescue. I wouldn't be here now if it wasn't for you. How did you know where I was?" Professor Jonas's eyes teared up as she lay her head back on the pillow.

Mariah took her hand and sat next to her bed. "Professor, when you didn't show up for our meeting after classes I knew something was wrong. Then we were worried sick when we found your car in the parking lot. Tony noticed your keys and suggested we look at the video of the parking lot. That's how we saw Professor Gyropolos hitting you over the head and dragging you to his car."

"I'm happy that you did! I thought I was going to die and no one would know where I was. I did put in a call to 911 and managed to say 'help' before my cell died. But no police came."

"Wait, you called 911 when you first got here? Well, that's why there was a police car next door at the warehouse. They must have received the wrong coordinates. Professor Gyropolos someone managed to kill them and bury them in his basement across from where he kept you."

"What? He killed two policemen while he had me in that room? I never heard anything. I guess I was out cold. He gave me a shot to put me to sleep."

"Professor Gyropolos mentioned killing the policemen while we were in the room with you. You were too busy trying to get out of your restraints to listen to him."

"Professor Jonas, please don't think about it now. It's over and he's in police custody. He can't harm you ever again," Tony declared.

"Yes, I guess you're right. I have to stop thinking about it. The police met me at the ER and took my statement. It's all so fresh in my mind but I still don't understand why he did it."

Mariah squeezed the professor's hand. "Who knows how a twisted mind works? He's crazy and nothing he does makes any sense, Professor. We are going to leave now so that you can rest. I don't want to see you getting upset."

"Thank you, Mariah, for everything. I think you should start calling me by my first name, Ellie. Okay?"

"Okay, Ellie. I'd like that. Now get some rest and I will call you tomorrow to see how you are doing. If you need a ride home I will come right over. Here's my number." Mariah wrote her number on the pad of paper that was on the end table next to the bed.

"See you later, Ellie. Sleep well."

"Thank you, Mariah and Tony, again for all that you did. I may call you if I don't have a ride home."

"Please do." Mariah and Tony waved and left the professor.

"Oh boy, she's in a bad way. I hope she gets some sleep tonight. Maybe they'll give her a tranquilizer to relax her."

"Most likely they will, Mariah. Let's get you home so you can sleep too. I'll pour you a glass of wine. That will relax you. I'll join you. I could use a drink!"

"Yeah, you can always use a drink, Tony!" Mariah smiled for the first time all day. She felt more relaxed after she saw Professor Jonas.

***

What Mariah didn't know was Sage was getting closer to finding out who he was.

CHAPTER TWENTY-FIVE

Two weeks passed quickly as Sherman gained in strength and had physical therapy to get his limbs working. He needed to continue doing stretching exercises since his muscles had been severely damaged. He was fortunate enough to be able to walk at all. He would have to continue with physical therapy once he left the hospital.

Arabella watched Sherman as he went through his routine of exercises slipping often as he adjusted his weight from one foot to the other. He used weights for his arms to build up the strength.

She would have to bring him into the hospital for physical therapy a few times a week unless she could find a physical therapy clinic closer to her home. It was forty minutes or more one way to the hospital from her house. She couldn't take off much time. She would try to take a week off when she took him to her home tomorrow and get him settled into a routine. Maybe she could look into getting a therapist to come to her home to make things easier for both of them.

Sherman acknowledged Arabella's presence from the doorway as she smiled back at him. He still hadn't spoken of his nightmares and they were increasing. Each night he woke up screaming.

The physical therapist settled Sherman into a wheelchair and brought him over to Arabella to escort him back to his room.

"How did you do today, Sherm?"

"Ah, it's tough…but I'm getting there…slowly. Have a lot more work to do yet. I will never walk…normally and always have a gimpy walk." Sherman's face scrunched up with a troubled expression. Because of all his scars, his face always looked like he was upset. But Arabella could see how he was feeling in his eyes.

"You are doing remarkably well, Sherman. Your speech has improved quite a bit too. You have a nice deep voice with a little rasp in it which is not at all harsh."

Once settled in his bed, Arabella left Sherman to check on other patients' orders. At the desk she would ask the doctor what time she could leave to take Sherman home the next day.

***

Sage lay back on his pillow and closed his eyes. He was exhausted from the strenuous exercises he had to do to regain the strength in his arms and legs. It would always hurt when he had to stretch them. It felt like an elastic that was being pulled tight and was in danger of springing back or breaking. He was determined to continue and get back as much as he could. He knew he would never be normal. *But what was normal for me anyway?*

Sherman thought back to his latest nightmare. He saw a cabin and a man lying with his head at an angle. He saw himself digging a hole and pushing the man into the hole. So far he had dreamt of a woman, a dog, and now a man. *Where was this? Could I have done these things? What kind of man am I?* Sherman shivered at the thought that he could be a killer. Maybe he shouldn't go home with Arabella. She could be in danger from him. He didn't know what he was capable of anymore.

Arabella came back to see him and announced, "Sherman, your dinner will be here shortly. I asked the doctor when we could leave tomorrow. After 11 am, Okay? I will take the rest of the day off and the week too. Another nurse will be covering for me. She owes me several days. Lucky for me."

"Okay. But, Arabella, I've been…thinking. Maybe I should go to…a hotel or somewhere. I will need to borrow some…money to do that. Then…I will look for a job."

"What are you talking about, Sherman. We decided you are going home with me. I'll make arrangements for a therapist to come to my house to work with you. Then you won't have to go out at all until you are stronger. When you do regain your strength I'll let you go out looking for a job. I don't want to hear any more about this. It's all settled."

"Boy, you're becoming a bossy woman, Arabella. We aren't even married," Sherman chuckled without moving his facial muscles too much since they hurt when he did.

Arabella blushed at the thought of marriage and gave Sherman her best smile. Maybe he was getting ideas, she thought.

Dinner was served and Arabella left Sherman once again to do some paperwork at the nurses' station. She needed to make notes for her replacement.

***

Sleep finally came for Sherman two hours after he had finished his dinner. He hadn't realized how exhausted he was. The nightmares kicked in once again and he was covered in blood. He thrashed and kicked trying to get away from it.

This dream appeared to be moving backwards and he once again saw the woman and dog, then he was running through the woods. He saw himself kicking and chopping at two large men outside what looked like a hospital. His hands were then handcuffed behind him and he walked backwards into the hospital with these two large men. He saw a man at the desk and heard the men asking to be let out of hospital. More people appeared as they continued to walk backwards – a doctor, an old woman, an old couple, a man and a young woman and another man appeared before him. They looked familiar – *but how would I know them? Who were they?*

Sage woke up with a jerk and realized that he did know them. He knew them all. They were his family and he wanted to kill them! He pulled off the sheets, sat up, and looked for his clothes. They were not in the locker. *Of course, they were destroyed by the bear.* He wrapped the sheet around him and left the room. He walked down the corridor until he came to a closet. He opened it and pulled out a pair of doctor scrubs and put them on. He noticed, on the shelf, a scalpel wrapped in plastic that someone had left there. He pocketed it for safe keeping. He may need that later. He hobbled along until he came to a locker room and found some man's shoes that had been left behind. As he was putting the shoes on, a man came out of the shower and tried to stop him saying, "What are you doing? Those are my shoes!" Sage knocked the man down, grabbed a bucket nearby and hit him on the head.

Sage continued to put on the shoes. They were a little big but he tied the laces tightly and shuffled out of the hospital as quickly as he could without being seen.

A short time later the man regained consciousness and alerted hospital security of the theft of his shoes.

Sage checked cars randomly in the parking lot until he found one that was unlocked and had keys under the front tire stuck to a magnet. *Stupid people who do this,* he thought. *Lucky for me that they do.*

He pulled away from the hospital and headed back to his brother's hospital where it all ended over a year ago. It shouldn't take too long to get there – an hour or so. Robert wouldn't be expecting him. That's the way he liked it. *Wouldn't he be happy to see me? He wouldn't even recognize me! Ha!*

Sherman, now Sage once again, drove as fast as he could and arrived within forty-five minutes at the Darien J. Roberts Psychiatric Hospital or Facility. Whatever they called it now. He would ask to see Dr. Roberts aka Dr. Fontana and say that he was in need of treatment.

Dan looked up when he saw an odd-looking man outside the slider motioning to be let in.

Dan pressed the speaker and asked the man, "Can I help you?"

"I need to see Dr. Fontana for treatment."

"Do you have an appointment?"

"Well, no but I'm sure he can make an exception and see me."

"One moment please, sir."

Dan quickly called Dr. Fontana and reported that a man asked for permission to see him.

"Who is it, Dan? Do you recognize him? Is it Sage?"

"I don't know. The man is severely disfigured and he's wearing scrubs. Maybe he's a doctor."

"Scrubs? Wait a minute. I'll be right down. I need to see him before you open the door."

Robert went to his safe and pulled out his gun. He didn't know whether to believe it could be Sage. It wouldn't hurt to have his gun with him, just in case. Maybe Sage had an accident, reason why we haven't seen him in over a year."

Robert walked over to Dan's desk and looked at the camera located at the front door. The man was looking directly at the camera and his face was so severely scarred that you couldn't tell if he was smiling or frowning. It was disturbing to look at.

"Dan, I'll go talk to him. Unlock it and then lock it behind me. I'll give you the signal when to open it again."

"Okay, if you're sure, Doc. I'll keep a watch. If you need help I can call the police pronto."

"No need of that yet. Let me see what he wants and who he is." Robert patted his pocket as he waited for Dan to open the slider. He walked outside and stood next to the disfigured man.

"What can I do for you, sir? Are you all right?"

"Yes, Doctor Fontana. I'm fine. How are you? It's been a long time, hasn't it?"

"Do I know you? Are you a doctor?"

"No! I can't believe you don't remember your own brother!"

"Sage, is that you? What happened to you and your voice? Why are you wearing scrubs?"

"Well, it's a long and sad story. But we have plenty of time to discuss it. Let me in and I will tell you all about my harrowing experiences since we were last together for our happy family gathering."

"I don't think we have anything to discuss, Sage. You are a wanted man by the police and the FBI. I wouldn't stay around here too long if I were you. Dan's calling the police now as we speak." Robert waved at Dan to call 911.

Dan nodded and picked up the phone and dialed never taking his eyes off of Dr. Fontana and the scarred man. Dan gave thumbs up to tell the doctor that the police were on their way.

Sage looked around him and hobbled back to his car but yelled out, "Hey Robert, I'm going to pay a visit to my sister, my mother and then Mariah if you won't let me stay here for a little while."

Robert panicked when he heard this and called Sage back. "You will not harm them, Sage. Do you hear me?" Robert pulled out the gun from his pocket and aimed it at Sage.

"Oh, I hear you, Big Brother, but I don't listen to you. I listen to a higher calling," Sage scoffed, "myself. Now, now, let's not be too hasty." Sage closed the distance between them when he saw the gun.

Even in his wobbly state Sage managed to grab the gun from Robert and twist it out of his hand before his brother knew what had happened.

"Now, let's go to your office and on your way by tell Dan to cancel the call to the police. Tell them you made a mistake and that everything is fine."

Robert hesitated but did as Sage told him when he saw the anger in Sage's eyes. Robert had no choice now that he had lost his gun. He would have to use his brain to come up with another way to stop Sage.

***

Back at the hospital, Arabella stopped by to check on Sherman but was shocked to find his bed empty. She went to the PT room in case he was there. Finding no one there she hurried back to the nurses' station to report him missing.

When she saw the doctor on call she asked, "Did you send the patient in 215 for tests or therapy? I went back to check on my patient and he was not there. I can't find him anywhere."

"Let me check his record and see if he was scheduled for any tests."

Arabella followed the doctor into the back room where the records were kept. He pulled out Sherman's file and scanned through it. "No, I don't see any tests that were scheduled here. In fact, he is going home tomorrow, isn't he?"

"Yes, that's why I'm upset. He should be in his room." Arabella didn't know where to turn. She didn't know where he could have gone. Sherman didn't even know who he was. *But, maybe now he does.*

***

Beatrice Fontana felt a tingling up and down her arms. She always got this feeling when one of her children were in some kind of danger. She grabbed her cell and called Robert. The phone rang and rang and finally went to voicemail. She called the hospital number and got Sharyn.

"Hi Sharynn, it's Beatrice. How are you? I've been trying to call Robert on his cell and he's not picking up."

"That's strange. He ran down to the lobby when Dan called a short time ago about a strange man wanting treatment."

"A strange man? What strange man? Where is Robert now?"

"He hasn't come back yet so I don't know anything about the man. Are you all right, Beatrice?"

"No, I don't like this not knowing who this man is. It could be Sage and if he comes in, Robert's life is in danger. You must call the police."

"Okay, Beatrice, calm down. Let me call Dan on the other line and find out what's going on. Okay? Hold on a minute. I'll get right back to you."

Dan picked up as soon as he saw it was Sharynn. "Hi Sharynn. What's up? Are you okay?"

"Where is Dr. Fontana? His mother is on the line and she's worried that something is wrong. What happened to that strange man that you called Dr. Fontana about?"

"Oh, Doc let him in and told me everything was okay and to cancel the police. But if you ask me, that man was a creature out of a horror movie. His voice was creepy too. I couldn't meet his eyes. I suggest you stay clear of him. But there was something familiar about his eyes. They remind me of... Oh my God! Sage! It's Sage! I better call the police and tell them right away. I need to hang up, Sharynn. I'll call you back later. Stay in your office and lock the door. I'll do a text code alarm to let staff know we are in lockdown and to stay alert."

"Oh no, I've got to get back to Beatrice. I better tell her too."

***

Mariah slept late and rolled over to talk to Tony but his side of the bed was cold. She wrapped her robe around her and pushed her feet into her slippers. Calling out to Tony, she walked toward the kitchen, "Where are you, Tony? Sorry I slept so late. Have you had breakfast yet?"

"Good morning sweetheart? How are you feeling? Rested? You did sleep late but I didn't want to disturb you. You needed the rest. I had coffee only. Sit down and I'll make us some eggs."

"Thanks, honey. I'm starving. Eggs sound good, toast please too."

"Of course, my love. Happy to hear that you are feeling better. If your appetite is back then my old Mariah is here."

"Well, almost here. I need to call Ellie at the hospital. I want to give her a ride home. She didn't call already, did she?"

"No, not yet. But I can go get her and you can rest and enjoy your day off."

"Absolutely not, Tony. I promised her I would come and get her and I always keep my promises."

"Okay, okay, Mariah. But sit down and have a cup of coffee and I'll take care of everything else in the kitchen. Eggs, toast, juice and bacon coming up!"

"Tony, I haven't heard from Uncle Robert in a couple of days. I have this funny feeling. I'll call him after breakfast too and see how he's doing."

"Yeah that would be a good idea. But I'm sure he would have called if Sage was found."

The phone rang as they were discussing Sage. Mariah picked it up and her face went white when she heard the shaky voice on the other end.

"Mariah, it's Gram."

"Hi Gram. How are you and Mom and Dad doing? I've been meaning to call you, but it's been crazy busy here. Are you all right?"

Tony watched Mariah's forehead wrinkle and her mouth open without a word being uttered as she listened to her Gram.

"I called Uncle Robert to talk to him. I had a strange feeling that something wasn't right. I couldn't reach him on his cell so I called Sharynn. She told me that Sage is there. He has been horribly disfigured from some kind of accident. He is with Robert now. Sharynn said that Dan called the police and they should be on their way there soon."

"Gram, I don't understand. What did you say? Oh my God, Gram. The nightmare is beginning again!"

"It's okay, Mariah. You are safe. He isn't coming there. Stay close to Tony and don't leave your apartment until I hear that the police have finally arrested Sage."

Mariah said goodbye to her grandmother and looked at Tony. "It's Sage, he's back! He's with Uncle Robert. We have to help him."

"No, you are not going anywhere. Did you forget that you have to pick up Ellie at the hospital? We'll go pick her up together after you eat your breakfast. Now eat! We will discuss Sage later. Let the police handle him." Tony's eyes flashed at Mariah.

"Okay, Tony. I'll eat but I will not even taste it. I am so enraged by the audacity of Sage to come back and go after Uncle Robert. I need to pray that the police will arrive in time to stop him before he harms my uncle." Under her breath Mariah whispered, *I will go help him.*

Mariah gulped down her coffee and breakfast and excused herself to shower while Tony cleaned up the kitchen and poured himself another coffee.

The phone rang and this time Tony answered. "Hi Ellie. How are you doing today? Are you ready to go home yet?"

"Yes, that's why I was calling. I don't need a ride. My parents are coming to get me. I called them and they want me to go to their house to stay until I feel up to going back to work. Tell Mariah thank you though for her offer to pick me up."

"Okay, Ellie. I will. Happy to hear that you will not be alone until you feel better. Mariah will call you soon. Can you give me the number where she can reach you?"

"Tell Mariah I will call her as soon as I am settled at my parents. Thanks again Tony for everything you and Mariah did for me. Bye."

"No need to thank me again. Take care, Ellie."

Tony turned to go tell Mariah that she didn't need to pick up Ellie when he heard the back door closing and her car starting up in the driveway. He grabbed his coat and ran out the door as Mariah backed her car out and sped away.

"Damn it, Mariah! What do you think you are doing?" He knew where she was going and called a cab to go to her Uncle Robert's hospital since his car was in the shop to be repaired. He silently recited a prayer that Mariah would be safe until he could get there.

CHAPTER TWENTY-SIX

Mariah pressed the gas pedal and raced to save her uncle. She hoped and prayed that she wasn't going to be too late. She had a gun now and would use it if the need arose. She and Tony had gone several times in the past two weeks to practice at the shooting range. She felt comfortable using it and proficient enough to shoot sure and straight.

She knew by the look on Tony's face that he was going to be coming after her soon. She may need his help too. Who knew what to expect when she arrived at the hospital. She had a long ride, over two hours, and didn't plan on stopping. It took almost as much time to get to her grandmother's in New Hampshire. She was in between her uncle's hospital and her grandmother's home.

Tony jumped into the cab and told the driver where he wanted to go. He promised an extra twenty-five dollars if the man got him there in less than two hours. Luckily Tony strapped himself in before the cabby raced away from his apartment.

***

Sage, with the gun in hand, sat across from Robert in the doctor's office. The odd fractured look on Sage's face looked like anything but a smile to his brother.

"Well, we have a lot to discuss and catch up on, don't we, Brother?" Sage put more emphasis on the word *brother* which was expressed in a derogatory tone.

Robert observed Sage and noticed that the only thing that had not changed on Sage were his eyes which were as steely and dead as a shark's. He shivered to think about what could have caused such horrendous injuries. Robert's heart skipped a beat in a moment of pity for his adopted brother but it was fleeting when he thought of what this man had done to many innocent women.

"Why so quiet, Robert? Don't you have anything to say? Haven't you been wondering what happened to me? I've been gone over a year now. Aren't you even curious?"

"Yes, I have been wondering what happened to you. I'm sure you are going to tell me though, aren't you?"

"Ha, it's a long story and some of it still is not clear to me, especially the bear attack."

"Bear attack? That was you? I heard about a man being attacked here in New York around Tambor Lake. How did that happened?"

"I was hiding out and hunting and got in the way of a hungry bear. My bad luck, huh?" Sage smirked and guffawed.

Robert looked horrified at the thought of what Sage endured. No one deserved that.

"I'm sorry you had to suffer like that."

"My, my, listen to you Brother! You actually are feeling sympathetic toward me? I never thought I would hear that in your voice. You have always treated me with disdain."

"Yes, but there was a reason for that. Look what you have done to so many women and their families. You have destroyed many families by taking their loved ones. You have to be punished for that. You have no regard for the meaning of life."

"Well, I wouldn't exactly say that, Robert. I regard my own life as important. I have a quest to fulfill and that is to destroy one more family before I am incarcerated. Our mother tried to destroy me by putting me in that hospital. I would still be there now and a vegetable like my natural mother if I hadn't escaped. I will never forgive her for that."

"Mother had to do what she thought was right for you. You were sick and still are."

***

Beatrice called Ronald to take her to her son's hospital. She told her daughter and son-in-law where and why she was going, "Betsy, I need to make sure that Robert is okay."

"Well, you're not going without us!" Betsy stated adamantly.

"I know you would say that. It's a four-hour drive but Ronald arranged to take us to the airport and get us there by a private plane in an hour. God bless him. He has a good friend who is a pilot and has his own plane. Ronald told him it was an emergency, which it certainly is."

"Thank God for Ronald. Time is of the essence. The sooner we get there the better. Hopefully the police will be there before we are. We should be there to support Robert no matter what happens."

***

"911, what's your emergency?"

"I'm calling from Darien J. Roberts Psychiatric Hospital. There's a man here that we think might be Sage, the one who is wanted by the police and FBI."

"What is your address? Do you have a description of this man?"

Dan told the operator his address and described the man the best way he could.

"You said he is severely disfigured and wearing scrubs?"

"Yes, but we think he is Sage. I saw his eyes and I will never forget those eyes from the last time he was here. He tried to kill Dr. Fontana then and I fear he will try again."

"A police car will be there shortly."

"Thank you." Dan hung up the phone but didn't feel that the operator believed him. His phone rang and brought him out of his reverie.

"This is Captain Kendall. Are you the one who called in an emergency about Sage?"

"Yes, I did. I didn't think the operator believed me. I know it sounded lame. But the guy is horribly disfigured and was wearing scrubs. I saw the man's eyes as he came into the hospital with Dr. Fontana. I know the Doc and could sense that he was disturbed by this man. Doc told me to call off the police. But I knew something wasn't right."

"I'll have my men there ASAP. Where is Dr. Fontana now?"

"He's in his office with the man. I haven't heard anything from him since."

"Detectives Armano and Snyder are on their way there now. Let them in. I'll have men surrounding the hospital. Can you get a message to Dr. Fontana?"

"I could try to contact him by text messaging."

"Ok, do that. Tell him what I told you. My men will keep in contact with me. The FBI will be sending men over too."

"All right, Captain. Thank you."

Dan texted Dr. Fontana and waited for a few minutes. He hoped the doctor would see it and feel relieved that help was on the way even if he couldn't acknowledge it.

Dr. Fontana could feel his phone buzzing in his pocket and slipped it out and glanced down to read the text from Dan. He sighed hoping the police would get there before Sage took his life.

"What you got there Robert? Would you like to share it with me?"

"No, it's my patients. I need to go check on them."

"Well, you will not be going anywhere without me. In fact, I think it's time that we left here and went to pay a visit to the rest of the family. Don't do anything stupid. Move slowly and head down to the basement. I know a quick way to get out of here without anyone seeing us."

***

Captain Kendall called in all his men and sent them toward the hospital. He also called the FBI Director Connor to alert him about the sighting. Captain planned on staying on the case until they were sure it was Sage.

"What's going on, Captain? Did you find Sage?" Director Connor inquired.

"We think it could be him. Got a call from Dr. Fontana's Lobby Attendant that a disfigured man came to see Dr. Fontana. He was wearing scrubs."

"Scrubs you say? That's strange. We received a call from New York Medical saying that one of their patients was missing. He was disfigured from a bear attack and possibly wearing scrubs or a hospital gown." Director Connor responded.

"What? It can't be? That man in the hospital all this time was Sage? You got to be kidding me?! Holy shit! No wonder we couldn't find him. He was right under our noses all this time! A whole year we've been looking for him. Why did they call you and not me?" Captain Kendall's voice quivered in disbelief.

"I've been watching and waiting for this man to wake up. I had a couple of my men check him out but the man couldn't remember who he was. The hospital reported the man was a John Doe and was scheduled to leave the hospital tomorrow. He was doing quite well considering his injuries. He had been in a coma for almost the whole year," Director explained

"Yes, I am well aware of that too, Director. My men visited with the man also without any luck. He didn't remember anything. They reported that the man was like a creature from a horror movie. He was that disfigured. Must have been an awful experience even for him. Maybe Sage got what was coming to him. But now he's back. Evidently he remembered who he was and what he wanted to do."

"I'm afraid you may be right, Captain. My men are heading that way now. We need to combine our efforts and not let Sage escape this time. If it is him. He doesn't have any next of kin from which to obtain DNA to verify his identity since his mother passed recently and was cremated."

"That is unfortunate. We will not let him get away, Director. I promise you that. You and I will have a drink – maybe two after this is all over."

"I think we will need them, Captain. Keep in touch. May God watch over all our men."

"Amen to that, Director."

CHAPTER TWENTY-SEVEN

Tony hung on as the cabby drove around 85-90 miles an hour on the highway and coming off the ramp took corners sharply. He sped along until he began to slow down upon entering the hospital parking lot.

He sighed in relief that they had made it safely. Tony thanked the cabby and gave him the fare plus the extra twenty-five dollars. The cabby certainly had earned it even if he had almost given Tony a heart attack.

He got out of the cab and looked around the parking lot. There were only a few cars there, probably the staff's cars.

Tony went up to the slider and buzzed for entrance. Dan's voice came on. "Can I help you?"

"Hey Dan, it's me, Tony Tremont. Can I come in?"

"Hi Tony. Sure, come on in. It's good you're here. We may need your help."

He sat next to Dan while he filled him in on what had happened. "Is Mariah here?"

"No, is she supposed to be here?"

"I expected her to be here before me. I guess the cabby really made good time. Where is Dr. Fontana and Sage now?"

"They're still in Dr. Fontana's office. It's been too quiet. I can't imagine what they're doing. I only hope Doc has his gun ready."

"I thought the police would be here by now. Did you call them right away?"

"Yes, I even spoke directly to Captain Kendall. He called me back when he received the call. He wanted to know if the man was really Sage. I told him I was positive by looking at his eyes. Captain was anxious to get his men here. The FBI are on the case too and their men are coming."

As Dan and Tony were talking, they could hear some activity outside. Dan looked at the cameras and could see several police officers and FBI agents moving forward to surround the building.

Two police were suddenly at the door buzzing to be let in. Dan opened the door to Detectives Armano and Snyder.

"Hi Dan, Tony. Is Sage really here? Where is he now?"

"He's with Dr. Fontana in his office."

"We need to get up there. Is there a way to get there without him knowing we're coming? Is there a back door to his office?"

"Yes, take the elevator up to the second floor and go directly to the office on your right. That's Sharynn's office. She will tell you where to go from there. I told her to lock her office door and stay put until you were here."

"Can you text her and let her know we are coming up. Tell her to be quiet and we will tap four times on the door so she will know it is us."

"Okay, Detective. Please keep her safe. She's important to me."

"We'll do our best, Dan. Don't worry. More police and FBI are following us. Let them in and tell them where we are. The place is surrounded. This should be over soon."

Dan sighed. "I certainly hope so, Detective."

Dan coded a lockdown which was delivered to everyone's cell and alerted Sharynn that the police were coming up and would use their secret knock. He also told her to contact Dr. Harper and let him know what was going on and that he would have to take over any problems with patients until Dr. Fontana was available.

Sharynn texted Dr. Harper. She knew that everyone would receive the coded lockdown as she had. But she called the kitchen to speak with Miguel in case he didn't have his cell on.

"Hi Sharynn."

"Did you get the code on your cell?"

"Yes, we are all in lockdown. Sage is here again? Can't believe that guy."

"I know, Miguel. Keep praying that this will be over soon."

"Will do, Sharynn."

***

After talking to Dan about hoping things would be over soon, Detective Armano whispered under his breath, "So do I."

Detective Snyder punched his arm and pushed him into the elevator. "What's wrong with you,

Armano? That's no way to promote confidence in the public."

"Yeah, but we know how Sage is. We have to be on our guard. We need as many police officers and FBI agents as possible to back us up."

The elevator dinged and several police and FBI agents spilled out to follow them. When they arrived at Dr. Fontana's secretary's office Det. Armano knocked four times. Sharynn appeared and seeing all the officers and agents, stepped aside to let them in.

"Is there a back door to Dr. Fontana's office?"

"Yes." Sharynn pointed the way past the bathroom and down another corridor. They crept along as quietly as several officers and agents possibly could. They listened outside the doctor's office and slowly turned the handle as they pushed the door rapidly inward. The office was empty.

***

Robert went downstairs to the basement with Sage close behind him. Sage was slow to negotiate the stairs and he held onto Robert to keep him close. He had the gun pressed tightly against Robert's back.

Robert's mind kept spinning trying to figure out his next step. He had to stay alive long enough to put an end to Sage's miserable life before he lost his own.

"Go to the right, Robert. There's a door there that will lead us to the back of the building and through a tunnel out to the street. I found it the last time I was here. I didn't get to use it but kept it right here." Sage tapped his head and continued, "I knew there would be another time when I would need it."

"I didn't know this tunnel was here? How did you find it?" Robert couldn't contain his curiosity.

"Ha, it was on the original blueprints. I got them online. You would be surprised how much you can get online nowadays."

"Hit that switch there before you enter the tunnel. It will light the way for us."

Robert did as he was told and wrapped his white coat closer around him. The tunnel was several degrees colder the deeper they traveled. Sage shivered too without a coat.

**

Mariah parked close to the front door of the hospital but was soon surrounded by several police as she tried to get out of her car.

The police opened her door and told her, "Get out of the car slowly. What business do you have here, ma'am? Who are you?"

Mariah held her hands up and pointed to her pocketbook in the front seat of her car. The officer reached in and picked it up for her. "Open it slowly and give me your identification."

Mariah obliged and handed her license to the officer closest to her. "I'm the niece of the director of this hospital, Dr. Robert Fontana. My name is Mariah Hampton. I'm here to see my uncle."

"You need to leave, ma'am. We are on police business. The whole hospital is off limits now."

"But I came to help my uncle."

"We know what to do, Mariah. You need to leave here immediately."

A few police officers began yelling, "He got away! He's not in the building. Scour the area around the garden in the back." Police officers and FBI agents ran in all directions trying to find Sage.

Now that the police and FBI were busy looking for Sage, Mariah ran over to the hospital door to buzz herself in.

She watched the police and FBI disperse, bit her lips and fisted her hands as she waited to get inside. She kept turning around to look behind her. Dan saw her coming and opened the door quickly.

"Hi Mariah. Tony said you were coming."

Turning to see Tony she exclaimed, "How did you get here before me?"

"Ha, didn't expect to see me here so quickly. It was quite a scary ride but I arrived safe and sound. It's not safe for you here. You shouldn't have come."

Mariah clipped sharply, "Never mind that now, Tony. Sage isn't here! The police and FBI are running all around looking for him. He got away!"

"What, what do you mean, he's not here now? Where did he go? How could he get out of the hospital without anyone seeing him?"

Dan stated, "Mariah, the police and FBI are upstairs now as we speak apprehending Sage in Doc's office."

The ringing of the phone stopped their conversation as they waited for Dan to pick up.

"Sharynn, are you all right? What happened?"

Mariah and Tony moved closer to Dan when they saw his face blanch.

"How did that happen? What? What did the police say?"

"You're kidding?"

As they waited to hear what happened, rumbling was heard coming from the stairwell where several police officers and FBI agents hurried into the lobby with guns drawn.

At the front of this group were Detectives Armano and Snyder who looked puzzled and were speaking to their Captain trying to calm him down as they announced, "Sorry Captain, we can't find him. He got away. We're canvasing the entire building floor by floor and Snyder and I are going down into the basement. He could be hiding out there."

Captain yelled loud enough for all to hear, "Get your asses down there and find him. Do you hear me, Armano and Snyder? There are no excuses!

You need to find him. I want him – I want him found now!"

"Yes sir, umm, we will find him, Captain." He had already hung up.

Detectives Armano and Snyder raced down to the basement with several other officers behind them. They could be heard yelling, "Clear! Clear!"

Outside was much the same as the officers scattered and ran around the building and into the woods to look for the illusive perpetrator once again.

Robert came to the road and stopped when Sage pulled him back. They came to a car that was parked nearby. Sage told Robert to get in.

He instructed Robert. "Take off your tie and hand it to me." Sage tied up Robert's hands with a few knots behind his back. Sage jumped into the car and drove away in the direction of their mother's house.

Robert could feel his phone vibrating again. He had tucked it inside his back pocket. He moved his hands around until he could reach his phone. Now all he had to do was somehow move it under him. He wiggled around until he managed to push his phone between his legs so he could look at it.

There was a text from his mother saying that she was on her way there to give her support. She was at the airport and coming in a limo with Ronald, Betsy, and Frank and would be there shortly.

Robert sighed heavily relieved that his family wouldn't be at the house when he and Sage got there. Robert knew he would have to make his move now.

Sage swerved the car to avoid hitting the policemen in the road ahead and he dropped the gun. The police opened fire at the car and Robert pushed himself down into the well as Sage ducked out of the way and raced ahead with the police and FBI following.

Mariah and Tony heard the gunshots and ran out to her car. Tony pushed Mariah into the front seat and steered out of the lot toward the sound of gun shots. He watched the police racing ahead and followed closely behind.

Mariah looked at her cell and texted her uncle. She didn't know what she would do if he didn't answer.

Robert stayed down in the well as gun shots rang out. He felt his phone vibrate under his knees and looked down at Mariah's text. "Are you all right?"

Robert could feel his heart pounding with each shot that was fired. Sage must have many lives left to have not been shot already, he thought.

"Tony, you have to get closer. Try going down that street and cutting Sage off," Mariah exclaimed.

Tony didn't respond but turned down the next street and came out in front of Sage. Mariah smiled but without any joy. She only wanted to get her revenge and see Sage captured but prayed that Uncle Robert would not be collateral damage.

Tony stopped the car dead in front of Sage's speeding car. Mariah, seeing what he was trying to do screamed, "Nooooo! Tony, don't!"

Tony turned the car out of the way at the last second, but this caused Sage to lose control of his car as he tried to apply the brakes. His car swung around in a circle and continued to spin out of control hitting a tree.

Police and FBI swarmed over the car as Tony and Mariah leaned in and pulled out Uncle Robert. Sage was unsteady but still alert.

Mariah looked at Sage and swung her fist connecting with his nose which now gushed with blood. Sage grabbed his nose and screamed at her,

"What the hell are you doing? Don't think for one minute I will forget this, Mariah."

"I hope you don't, Sage. I owed you more than that for what you did to my friend, Amanda. I hope you rot in prison for life. You deserve no less. You are the scum of the earth. I can't believe that there is another one like you. But we outsmarted him too!"

"Ha ha, you are so dramatic, Mariah! What do you mean – another one like me?"

"Oh, one day you will hear about him. Maybe you will both be in the same prison and can become bosom buddies," Mariah exclaimed as her eyes narrowed and she gritted her teeth. If the hatred and disgust she felt could kill, Sage would be dead now.

Mariah turned from Sage when Tony and Uncle Robert pulled her away from the car. The FBI and the police ushered them to the side of the road while they grabbed Sage and put him in handcuffs.

Tony yelled over to them, "Be careful. Check him for a pin."

Sage smiled at Tony's remark.

Detectives Armano and Snyder along with two FBI agents patted Sage down and thoroughly checked him for any pin or any other weapon. They pulled out a scalpel from his front pocket and found a handgun on the seat and bagged them for evidence.

Robert spoke up, "Hey Detectives, that's my gun. Sage took it from me."

"Okay, Doctor. You'll get it back after the investigation is complete."

"Never mind, I don't want it back. I don't think I will need it again."

The detective nodded back.

Detective Armano saluted Tony and lead the way for them to go back to the hospital while the FBI took Sage away.

Detective Snyder called into the station and reported what had transpired to Captain Kendall.

"We got him, Captain! We got him!"

"All right! Wonderful news, men! Thank you! Where's Sage now? Did the FBI take him away? Did you see him in handcuffs in their car?"

"Yes, he's getting into the car now and he is handcuffed. They thoroughly checked him over for weapons or pins. He had a scalpel on him. There was also a gun found in the car which belonged to Dr. Fontana but nothing else."

"Good to know. I'll have to talk to Director Connor. I'm sure he heard from his men already but I want to gloat. You guys did it, right?"

"Yes, Captain, we did. We were first on the scene when his car crashed. Also, we can thank Tony and Mariah for causing the crash. I guess they finally got their revenge."

"Well, not yet, Detective, until Sage is put behind bars for good. Then, I too, will be happy."

Tony and Mariah went back to get her car, Mariah told Tony she would be following the FBI and Sage to make sure they got him. There's no way she would allow him to get away again. She had a funny feeling that the agents had no idea who they were dealing with. But she did! She patted her pocket where the gun was safely tucked.

"Mariah, wait. I'll come with you!" Tony jumped in beside her before she could drive away. The FBI vehicle was up ahead stopped at a light but something was wrong. The light changed and they didn't move.

Mariah got out of her car and walked up to the agents' vehicle to see why they weren't moving. As Mariah got closer she saw Sage using his cuffs to choke an agent. One was unconscious already. Mariah pulled out her gun from her pocket and aimed it at Sage through the car window.

Sage released the unconscious agent from his grip and got out of the car and ran or more like wobbled away.

Mariah ran after him as Tony followed close behind yelling, "Mariah don't do it. Wait for me."

Mariah yelled back, "Sorry, Tony, but I have to end this now."

Sage couldn't move fast. He hobbled along with his hands still in cuffs which he had managed to move in front of him.

Mariah called out, "You can't go far, Sage. I will shoot you in the back if I have to."

"You probably can't hit an elephant right in front of you." Sage laughed but kept moving forward into the treed area.

"Don't be too sure of that."

Sage ducked into the woods and used the trees as cover. But Mariah would not be deterred. She was determined to kill Sage and no one, not even Tony, could stop her.

CHAPTER TWENTY-EIGHT

Director Connor tried to contact his men. He hadn't heard from them for well over an hour. He had told them to keep in touch with him as they headed to the office of Captain Kendall. He was going to keep Sage there until he could move him to the FBI's New York Office.

Captain Kendall called Director Connor. "Have you heard from your men yet? I have a cell warmed up for him," Captain snorted.

"Hmm, thank you, Captain. But Sage won't be staying long. I plan to move him first thing in the morning. I will have my men keeping a watch over him until then. I expect to hear from my men soon. When they arrive there let me know. Talk to you later, Captain."

"Okay, Director." Captain noticed the angst in the Director's voice. He only hoped that the FBI agents would deliver Sage without any problems arising. But he felt the hairs on the back of his neck tingling and didn't like it.

***

Beatrice and her entourage arrived at the hospital to chaos. There were police cruisers scattered around along with FBI vehicles. They hesitated to get out of the cab, but Ronald assured them that they were probably safer inside than outside in case Sage was on the grounds.

Beatrice texted her son to let him know they were at the hospital. She received a text back saying, "Come right in. Sage is on his way to the Lindan Police Station."

Ronald escorted the ladies along with Frank into the hospital. Hugging the women and shaking hands with the men Robert smiled. "Hi everyone. Nice to see you. But it wasn't necessary for you to come."

"Maybe, but we couldn't let you deal with this on your own. We came to give you our support but evidently we're too late. But not too late to spend some time with you. Thank God Sage is going to be put away for good. So, what and how did it happen?"

Robert invited them into the dining room and had Miguel prepare dinner for everyone while he explained in detail what had transpired with Sage. He left out the fact that Mariah and Tony were the cause of Sage's car accident.

"Thank goodness you are safe. Now where are Mariah and Tony?"

"Well, they raced out of here. I guess they wanted to get back home." Robert left out that he knew Mariah was following the agents to make sure that they delivered Sage to the New York Police Station. He prayed the agents did their job and Mariah and Tony would return to the hospital to tell him about it.

***

Director Connor couldn't reach his agents and now had to send two more agents to find them. He called the men that were already at the hospital to find the missing agents and Sage with the order, "Call me as soon as you find them. I want Sage. I don't care what you do, get him and bring him to the New York Police Station."

The four agents raced off to find their fellow agents and Sage, determined to do their best.

Director knew it was time to call Captain Kendall. He didn't look forward to hearing about how incompetent his men were once again.

"Captain, I haven't heard from my men but I'm sending out four more men to find them. They could have had car trouble. When I know more I will contact you."

"What? Not again! I think you need to find some more reliable men. Do you want to borrow some of my finest?" Captain tried not to snicker because he was angry and not happy about Sage being possibly on the loose again.

"Listen, Director. I will keep my men at your disposal. I'm not happy to hear that Sage may have gotten the better of your men. I pray that they are alive. Keep in touch. If they do arrive here I will call you immediately."

"Thank you, Captain. I appreciate that."

Saying "thank you" to the police was always a difficult thing. Director Connor felt the words were foreign to him. He never thanked anyone until now. He found that he was depending upon the local authorities too much for his own liking. The FBI didn't do that. He had to get this man in custody or his reputation would slide downward and he could lose his job. *Damn that Sage!*

***

Mariah stopped and listened but couldn't find Sage. The trees were thick here, the light was waning and the temperature was dropping. She buttoned up her coat and moved quickly forward. *How could Sage have disappeared? He could barely walk.*

Tony caught up with Mariah and pulled her aside. "Mariah, let's go back to the car and call the police. You can't do this alone. It's getting colder and you aren't dressed warm enough to stay out too long."

"Oh, Tony, I'm not a baby! I'm warm enough. After all, Sage doesn't even have a coat on – only scrubs. I'm going to find him. Now, you can come with me or go back to my car and call the police for backup."

Tony sighed, shook his head and nodded. "Okay, Mariah. I'm going with you. Do you have your gun and enough bullets?"

"Ha ha funny man. I don't need many but I do have enough." Mariah showed her gun to Tony and pulled out the sleeve of bullets from her pocket.

"Okay, I believe you, Mariah, but be careful. I will be right here with you. But I need to call the police to find what's going on. Where in Hell is the FBI?"

Tony pulled up Captain Kendall's direct number and waited for him to pick up. "This is Tony. Sage escaped again. Mariah and I followed behind the

FBI vehicle. We saw Sage choke the agents and flee into the woods. We are going in after him."

"No, Tony! I'll send some men there to search for him. Take Mariah and go back to her uncle's hospital where you will be safe. I need to call Director Connor now. Stay away from Sage. I'll call you back shortly. You had better be at the hospital by then. No sense putting both of you in danger."

"I can't hear you, Captain. We must be losing the signal. I need to go." Tony abruptly pressed end on his phone before Captain could say anything else.

He knew he would have to pay for disobeying the Captain. He had to make a choice who to listen to – Mariah or Captain Kendall. There was no choice here. He moved forward deeper into the woods and pulled out his flashlight that was attached to his house keys.

Tony whispered, "Mariah, where are you?"

He moved the light back and forth trying to locate Mariah and Sage. He saw movement ahead and Sage crouched down behind a large tree.

A gun shot rang out and Sage moved away. Tony looked around and called out, "Mariah, where are you?"

Mariah came out of hiding when she heard Tony's voice. "Tony, I almost hit you! Now he got away again!"

Mariah had her own flashlight and pointed in the direction that Sage had taken. She took off again after him. "Stay out of my way, Tony. I'm going to get him. I'm going to kill him for Amanda and all the other women he murdered. He will never go to prison."

"Mariah, please wait for the police. They're on their way."

Mariah continued forward and didn't acknowledge Tony's plea.

Sage listened to their conversation and crawled around looking for a place to hide. He shivered and tried to keep warm. He knew that he wouldn't survive unless he found a place to warm up. There were some buildings further into the woods. Looked like a warehouse and an abandoned shack. He hobbled closer and hid behind another tree. As he got closer he made a slow run for it. The door of the shack was unlocked. Without a light he couldn't see much and felt his way around until he stumbled over a bed. He hid underneath and pulled the dusty old covers over him. He was shivering uncontrollably now and tucked the covers around him snuggly to try to get warm.

Mariah and Tony kept walking around and came up to the shack and what looked like a warehouse. They crept forward and beamed their flashlights around the area.

Mariah tried the door of the shack and turned the handle which nearly came off in her hand. Tony went around the back and checked for a door. He looked inside the window with his light and saw a bed against the wall with the covers on the floor. No sign of Sage. There was some furniture piled up in the opposite corner but nowhere for Sage to hide that he could see.

Mariah pushed open the door and moved her light back and forth. She saw a mess of broken down furniture piled up in one corner of the room and a bed in the other. The covers appeared to be piled up under the bed.

She moved closer to look under the pile. She kept her gun out in front of her and the light sweeping back and forth.

Mariah wasn't prepared for what happened next.

***

A few of the police officers and FBI agents, who were at the hospital, drove to find the agents and Sage once they received word from their Captain and Director. When they arrived at the light they saw a car and an FBI vehicle parked there. The men looked inside the vehicle and saw two FBI men unconscious. The police put in a report to Captain Kendall and the agents reported to Director Connor and called for an ambulance for the two unconscious agents.

The police officers and FBI agents fanned out throughout the woods and followed the path that was made by Mariah, Tony and Sage. Branches were broken off and leaves were trampled. There wasn't much snow left due to some melting the day before. Footprints could still be seen in what snow was left all going in the same direction.

Detectives Armano and Snyder led the way until they reached the shack and warehouse. They saw some flashlights moving back and forth inside the shack and headed that way.

A gunshot rang off followed by three more. Racing forward, the police and agents surrounded the shack and broke down the door.

Mariah stood over Sage while Tony held onto his injured right arm. Mariah held her gun as she turned toward the police officers and FBI agents.

Detective Snyder stepped forward. "Mariah, put down the gun slowly and step away from Sage."

As Mariah lowered her gun, Detective Snyder guided Mariah, clearly in shock, away from Sage.

Detective Armano moved to Tony and wrapped his coat around Tony's arm which bled heavily.

The agents bent over Sage and felt his pulse. He was still alive but had three wounds, one in his groin and the others in both knees.

It was evident Sage could not move on his own. The two agents pulled him to his feet and dragged him along to their vehicle. It was rough going through the woods and Sage grunted and groaned his way through. The agents didn't notice his discomfort or were intentionally ignoring him.

Tony wrapped his good arm around Mariah and led her back to her car. Sage was being picked up by an ambulance with four of the agents accompanying him there. They were not going to let him out of their sight per request of Director Connor.

Tony was being brought to the hospital for treatment along with Mariah who was still in shock. They were concerned about her car but were assured by the police that Mariah's car would be taken back to the hospital for safe keeping.

Detectives Armano and Snyder arranged for an ambulance and escorted them to the hospital. Another ambulance had already picked up the two unconscious agents. The Detectives needed to obtain Mariah's and Tony's version of what happened at the shack. Captain Kendall wanted to know exactly what happened and why.

***

Director Connor was relieved to hear that his men had apprehended Sage and brought him to the hospital from which he had previously escaped. His injuries were not life threatening but would definitely keep him off his feet for a long time.

Tony was recovering and so was Mariah. She finally was talking and sat by his bed and held his hand.

The two detectives were standing nearby as she began to relive her experience.

CHAPTER TWENTY-NINE

Mariah took a deep breath and began her story.

"I bent down to look at the lump under the bed when it suddenly moved. Sage uncovered himself, kicked out at me, and tried to knock me down. Sage startled me and caused my gun to go off and I accidently shot Tony."

Tony sighed. "It hurt like hell. It was quite a shock. One minute I was there to back up Mariah and the next I was down on my knees in pain."

After seeing Mariah's tear-streaked face Tony added, "It's okay, Mariah. It was an accident. I'll live. The bullet didn't hit anything crucial. I will have to be taken care of. That's all." Tony smiled at Mariah but winced as he tried to move his arm.

"What happened next, Mariah?" Detective Snyder probed to get her back on task.

"I held onto the gun and aimed it at Sage who was still on the floor trying to get up. As he came closer to me I shot him in the groin. But he still came toward me and reached out to grab the gun away from me. I shot him in one knee then the other when he continued to come at me."

Mariah shivered not from the cold but from remembering that she had shot two people – one that she loved, and the other one that she hated.

But now, finally, she felt that she had avenged her friend, Amanda's life.

"Tony, we need to corroborate this. Do you have anything to add?" Detective Armano queried.

"No, I went down as soon as I was shot but did see Mariah do exactly what she reported she did. Sage tried to attack her and grab the gun. She did what she had to do and shot him again. I'm sorry I dropped my gun when I was shot. Otherwise I might have shot him myself."

"Okay, you two. Do you want a ride back to Dr. Fontana's hospital?" Detective Snyder offered.

"Yes, please. We want to get back home but would like to visit with my uncle and get a bite to eat. He's going to want a full report. We may stay there for the night."

"That's fine too. We'll know where to contact you in case we need more information after talking to the Captain. He may want to talk to you directly," Detective Armano responded and led the way to his police car to escort them back to Darien J. Roberts Psychiatric Hospital.

Once back at the Psychiatric Hospital, Mariah and Tony were welcomed with open arms by her whole family much to her surprise.

"What are you all doing here?"

"Well, we couldn't stand by and not be here for your Uncle Robert," Grandmother Beatrice declared.

"Isn't that why you and Tony came?" Mariah's mother, Betsy inquired.

"Yes, Mom, I guess we think the same way."

Tony looked serious and announced, "Mariah and I have to tell you what happened."

Robert stepped forward when he saw Mariah's troubled face and Tony was grimacing in pain and wearing a bandage and sling around his right arm. "What happened to you two? Where did you go? You've been gone a long time and your car is back out in the lot and you didn't drive it here."

"Well, that's what we want to clarify for you." Tony continued to explain.

Mariah added her own description of how she had shot Tony and Sage.

Beatrice wrapped her arms around Mariah who looked like she was going to pass out from exhaustion and shock. "Oh my dear Mariah! I can't believe you did that? I'm not saying it was a bad thing to do to Sage but to shoot Tony! That must have shocked you."

"Well, I think it hurt me more than it did Mariah, Mrs. Fontana." Tony tried to laugh and ease the tension but grimaced when his pain increased.

"Oh my God, Gram, I couldn't believe I did that! But it was an accident. I would never do that intentionally. Sage put me off balance when he tried to kick my legs out. The gun went off and Tony was in the wrong place at the wrong time. Sorry, Tony." Mariah, with tears brimming in her eyes, looked sheepishly at him.

"It's all forgotten, Mariah. You did what you had to do and that's what's important here. You finally got him! Now we can rest."

Her mother, father and uncle hugged Mariah. She was surrounded by her family which was the best place to be.

"Are you okay, Mariah?" Her mother touched Mariah's face and kissed her cheek.

"I'm fine, Mom. Don't worry. It's all over. It's finally over," Mariah sighed and tears cascaded freely, providing a much needed release.

***

Sage lay on a bed in the emergency room with the four agents standing next to his bed as the doctors and nurses hovered over him. The doctors were going to move Sage to the operating room to remove the bullets and repair the damage.

A shuffling could be heard as a woman in white ran into the ER and screamed out – "Sherman! Where are you Sherman?"

She came up to the doctors as they were moving the patient away. She gripped the bar of the bed to prevent them from moving forward. She looked closely at the patient and took note of his injuries. "Sherman, what happened to you? Why did you leave?"

Sage shook his head, clearly in immense pain, but didn't answer.

Arabella, feeling dejected, released her grip on the bed and stepped aside as the doctors pushed past her. She called out to the patient, "I'll be waiting for you after surgery, Sherman. We can talk then."

The four agents weren't allowed inside the OR but stayed close by and called Director Connor to report that Sage was now in surgery.

"I want you men on top of him when he comes out of surgery. You don't leave his room for a minute. If you have to leave, I want three of you there at all times. I want to know every move he makes once he is awake."

"Yes sir," the agent answered and relayed to the other agents what Director had told him.

An hour later Sage was settled in a room with the four agents by his bedside. Sage had not woken up yet. But they were not moving any time soon.

A nurse came into the room and told the agents, "You need to leave the room while I take the patient's vitals and check his sutures."

"We are not going anywhere, ma'am," one agent announced and added, "that's our orders."

"Okay, but I hope you have good stomachs because this is not going to be pleasant."

The agents exchanged wary looks and shook their heads. "Sorry, Ma'am, we aren't going anywhere."

Arabella pulled Sage's covers off of him so the agents could see his severely mangled legs. She took his vitals and examined his sutures as the agents stoically looked on.

Arabella smiled to herself as she continued to expose more of his damaged body to the agents. She tried to force the agents from the room, but to no avail. They were used to much more.

Sage stirred and looked up to see Arabella smiling down on him.

"Sherman, how are you feeling?" Arabella covered him up and smoothed out his covers.

Sage opened his eyes and looked groggily at her. "How the hell do you think I feel? I was shot in both knees and in my privates. I will get even with that woman!" He groaned as he tried to move.

Arabella couldn't believe that this was the same man that she was beginning to have feelings for. *What happened to change him like this?*

"Sherman, what happened to you? Who did this?"

"Who's Sherman, I'm not Sherman. Who the hell is Sherman?"

"My name is Sage. Why are you calling me Sherman?"

Arabella flinched, turned away from the patient and swiftly left the room. She didn't want him to see her tears. The man in that bed was no longer her Sherman. Arabella planned on finding out who did this to her Sherman and why. She would make them pay!

***

Tony and Mariah sat quietly after dinner and continued to answer questions from her family. They were all in awe over what Mariah had done to Sage.

Robert checked over Tony's arm, put it in a fresh sling, and gave him a pain killer so he could sleep. Tony had refused to stay overnight in the hospital, saying that he was going to his friend's hospital to spend the night.

Robert also offered to give Mariah a tranquilizer. She was still looking pretty shaky. But she refused it, saying that she wanted a clear head.

Robert had spoken to Captain Kendall a short time before and learned that Sage was being operated on to repair the damage that Mariah had inflicted upon him.

"If we are lucky, Sage will never walk nor will he be able to rape any woman again."

"He deserves no less, Captain, for what he has done."

"Yes, Doc, but we can't put our guard down yet. Sage is a slippery fellow. How's Mariah and Tony doing?"

"They're okay. Tony's a little sore. Mariah is still in shock but I will be watching her closely. They will stay here tonight. Both will be under my care."

"That's good to hear, doctor. Well, take care of them. Keep your fingers crossed that this is finally over."

"I will, Captain. Good night."

Captain ended one call and began another. Director Connor was still in his office too and had, a few minutes before, spoken to his men at the hospital who were guarding Sage.

"How's our perp doing?"

"Sage came out of surgery and is doing well. His knees were shattered by the bullets and he may never walk again. As for his groin, well, let me put it this way. He will not be fathering any children ever, thanks to Mariah."

"Yes, I heard that, Director. Mariah is quite a young woman. She's got a lot of guts. She was determined to make Sage pay for killing her friend. She did it!" Captain agreed.

"Now we need to get Sage moved as soon as possible to a more secure location. We don't trust him even in the state that he is in right now."

"I agree, Director. Well, keep me posted. Good night."

***

Arabella was determined to find out about Sherman's injuries. She refused to call him anything but Sherman no matter what he told her.

Arabella met with the doctor on call and reviewed his chart. It showed that Sherman had been shot in his groin and both knees. But who did it and why?

The chart didn't say anything more about how and why it happened. But she was determined to find out. Arabella wasn't about to let Sherman go. She had seen inside his heart and there was a kindness there that would come out again if only she could help him.

***

Sage slept fitfully through the night and when he opened his eyes it was still dark outside. He could see the outline of four shapes in the corners of his room. The agents were still there. *Didn't they eat or sleep?*

He was trapped in this bed, couldn't move even if he wanted to. His knees were shattered by the bullets shot by that bitch. He was going to need help to get out of here. His only hope would be that crazy nurse with the nice eyes, Arabella. She had grandiose ideas about the two of them. It was not going to happen! But he would use her and then toss her away. He would draw the line at killing her since she did care for him, not only because she had to in her job, but also in her heart.

Sage got a twinge of pain as he tried to move but also felt something else. He laughed over the fact that he could even fathom having feelings for Arabella too. He tossed aside these thoughts. He couldn't act on that for it would be the last of him. One woman nearly killed him and now another could break him completely. He had to keep his guard up. Too many women in his life could destroy him - first his adoptive mother, then Mariah, and now Arabella.

The agents stirred and looked directly at Sage. One agent came closer to his bed and leaned in. Sage closed his eyes and pretended to be asleep. The agent moved away and woke up the other agents to be on alert. "He's awake. Stay alert, men. I'm going to get us some coffee and bagels. We can take bathroom shifts. I'll call Director in a few to check in. He will tell us what to do next."

The three agents, still groggy from sleep, nodded and grunted in assent as he left the room. While the agent was waiting for the coffee and bagels at the cafeteria he called Director Connor.

"Director, Agent Bush checking in, Sir. The patient is awake. He slept fitfully last night. I heard him moaning in pain. I'm a light sleeper myself."

"Listen Agent Bush, are you in the room now?"

"No, I'm in the cafeteria getting us some breakfast. We didn't get to eat last night."

"Well, hurry up and get back to that room. When you see the doctor tell him we need to move the patient ASAP. If he says no, we move him anyway. I'll send a doctor there to escort the patient along with the four of you to a discreet location."

"Yes, Sir," Agent Bush responded as he paid, grabbed the coffees and bagels, and hurried back to Sage's room.

When he arrived, the nurse was at the patient's bedside talking softly to him. He listened in to try to catch what she was saying. He caught these words. "...I'll   help   you...no   problem...my house...today...later."

Agent Bush spoke softly to the other agents, "I spoke to Director and he is sending a doctor here to escort the patient along with us. We are leaving with the patient as soon as the FBI doctor gets here. I don't like that nurse. She is too chummy with the patient. I listened to her when she spoke to Sage and heard her mention that she will help him and possibly take him to her house later. We need to move before she tries something. Evidently she has no idea who she is dealing with."

An agent spoke up, "I agree. She came in right after you left. She is definitely conspiring to help him escape. Sage is cagey and has convinced her that he is sane."

"Drink up your coffees, agents, and eat your bagels. They may be all you'll get to eat for a while."

All nodded in agreement as they chewed and swallowed quickly never taking their eyes off of the patient and the interfering nurse.

Sage whispered back to Arabella. "When will you come back to get me?"

"As soon as I finish with a few other patients and get someone to cover me for the rest of the day. I will take you down to my car on the bed and move you to a wheelchair when we get to the parking garage door. We always leave a few chairs there for patients."

"Thank you, Arabella. I couldn't do this without you."

Arabella smiled and leaned over Sage and planted a kiss on his scared cheek which caused Sage to scrunch up his face into a grimace of a smile.

Sage quickly composed himself so as not to relay any emotion toward Arabella. But Arabella could see the emotion in his eyes and smiled.

The agents watched this exchange and stood up and formed a barrier to the door preventing Arabella from leaving.

"What do you think you are doing? I need to see to other patients. You're in my way."

"No problem, ma'am, let me escort you out of the room," Agent Pressor declared. He opened the door and followed her into the hall.

He put his hand on her elbow to stop her. "Ma'am, you need to stay away from this patient. He is under arrest. He will leave this hospital and you will not get in the way. Do you understand? He was a fugitive and was finally caught. Let me tell you about him."

Arabella listened as Agent Pressor told her as much as he was safe to share about Sage's exploits. Her eyes widened in shock and she cringed as she thought over what her Sherman had done. It couldn't be true!

"You must have the wrong man. Sherman couldn't do those things you say that this man, this fugitive, you spoke about, did. This is not Sherman."

"Oh, ma'am, we are definitely sure about this fact. You call him Sherman, but he is really Sage. He is not to be trusted. He nearly killed members of his own family twice. It was fortunate that his niece shot him first."

Taking in a sharp breath, Arabella relaxed now knowing who had shot her Sherman. She was determined to go after this woman and make her pay for what she did to him.

"Are you listening to me, ma'am? This is in FBI jurisdiction and you need to stay out of the way or you will be arrested for obstruction of justice."

"I understand. Now let me go. I need to see the rest of my patients," Arabella scoffed while she silently thought over what she would do next.

Agent Pressor moved aside but kept an eye on Arabella as she traveled down the corridor and went into another room. He went back in to confer with his fellow agents.

"What did she say, Agent Pressor?" Agent Bush queried.

"She didn't disagree with me but I could see the wheels turning as she was planning what to do next."

"Okay, we need to move now. I'll call Director Connor and let him know about this new development," Agent Bush announced.

CHAPTER THIRTY

Mariah had a fitful night with little sleep. She dreamt about shooting Tony and Sage. She watched it play out over and over again.

She still couldn't believe that she had shot Tony. Poor guy. He never complained after it happened. He tried to make Mariah feel better by saying it was okay, only an accident. She didn't think she could be as forgiving if it had been her being shot by him.

Mariah showered and dressed and went next door to Tony's room to see how he was doing. But Tony's bed was empty.

Mariah went out into the dining room to see if maybe he was having breakfast. Her family were all there, including Tony, who was holding his arm protectively as he got up to greet Mariah.

"How are you, Mariah? Did you sleep well?"

"Tony, it should be me asking you how you slept. Did you sleep okay?"

"Yes, Mariah, I slept fine. Your uncle gave me some pain killers that really worked. My arm is stiff and sore but better thanks to him."

"Will you regain full range of motion with your arm, Tony?"

"Well, the doctor said I may experience some permanent stiffness when I try to lift it straight up. But I may need some PT to strengthen it. Nothing vital was injured there. It was an in and out shot. Which is a good thing. I'm not worried about it, Mariah, and you shouldn't be either."

Mariah sighed but couldn't keep the tears out of her eyes. "Okay, Tony, but you know I will worry about you until it is all healed and you are throwing flying disks again."

"Flying disks? When did I ever throw a flying disk?" Tony was puzzled as he looked at Mariah's smirk.

"What are you up to, Mariah?"

"Well, I've been thinking, Tony."

"Ooh, that's dangerous, Mariah!" Tony chuckled.

"Let me explain, funny man! I've been thinking that after I finish school I want to get a dog, a large dog. You know the kind, for protection. Then you can learn to throw flying disks to him or her."

"Hmm, interesting, Mariah. I think I would like that. I haven't had a dog since I was a little boy. I had a yellow lab. Great dog! He loved to play catch and pull the rope. Sounds like a good idea, Mariah. He would also be protection for you."

"Oh good. I was afraid you wouldn't agree. It would be good protection for both of us when we start a family."

"Yes, but we need to get married first. As soon as you complete your degree we will tie the knot, I promise, Mariah."

"Is this a proposal, Tony?" Mariah grinned, happy that she had tricked him into proposing.

Mariah's family listened to their conversation and clapped. They began chanting, "Propose to her. Propose to her!"

"Okay, okay, people. I need the ring first before I can do that."

Beatrice pulled off her ring and handed it to Tony. "Now there is no excuse. I want Mariah to have my ring. I only continued to wear it until she needed it."

Tony took the beautiful three carat diamond with smaller diamonds on each side and got down on one knee.

Mariah, seeing him on his knee, began to cry. Betsy handed Mariah a tissue and patted her on the arm.

Everyone waited while Tony composed himself too. He was in danger of tearing up by seeing Mariah in tears.

"Mariah, will you please do me the honor of being my wife? I love you now and will love you forever."

Mariah put her hand out to receive the gorgeous ring and cried out in a choked voice, "I will, Tony! I will be your wife and love you forever too."

Tony slipped the diamond ring onto Mariah's finger and raucous clapping began as Tony hugged and kissed Mariah, holding her close with his one good arm as she continued to cry.

Everyone surrounded the happy couple and congratulations rang out loud and clear.

Tony looked around and thought to himself, I was suckered into this. Boy I can't believe it! But I am happy I did it. I couldn't live without her.

Mariah showed off her new ring to everyone and gripped her grandmother in a tight hug to say thanks for the lovely surprise gift.

"Thank you, Gram. Your ring is beautiful! I always admired it. It's a perfect fit too!"

"Yes, dear Mariah, I know you did. I have been waiting for this moment to give it to you. And now it is yours! Enjoy it and may it bring you both much happiness as husband and wife. I also want to give you another gift, Mariah and Tony."

Tony looked up in surprise. "Another gift, Beatrice? What more can you possibly give us? The ring is way more than I could ever afford. Thank you for that. You made Mariah happy."

"You are welcome, Tony. But it isn't me who makes Mariah happy. It is you! Now let me continue. I have a house that is five miles away from my larger house. I bought it many years ago and have kept it in good condition. Ronald has taken care of that for me. Bless him. It has three bedrooms and two and a half baths, living room, dining room and country kitchen and a large finished basement for the kids one day. It also has a two-car garage. It is all furnished and everything in it is yours when you are married."

Tony and Mariah exchanged shocked looks and recited together, "Thank you, Gram! Thank you, Beatrice!"

"Oh, you are welcome, dears. And Tony, now you will be calling me Gram too."

"Umm, okay, Gram. Thank you! This is more than we could ever hope for. You are much too generous, Gram. I owe you big time for all you have done."

"Oh, nonsense, you are family or will be soon, young man. Come on over here and give me a hug and I will consider that payment enough." Gram put her arms out to Tony and carefully hugged him leaving his bandaged arm in a sling away from her.

Robert left the room and went to see Miguel. "Hey, Miguel. We have a special occasion to celebrate. Do you have any champagne or wine or anything sparkly?"

"What's going on, Doc? Did I miss something?"

"Yes, sorry I should have gone to get you but it happened too quickly. Tony proposed to Mariah!"

"Wow, is that right? And I missed it? Wait, I have the perfect thing." Miguel pulled out a bottle of wine that he had put aside to use for cooking. It was a Portuguese wine, a port.

"Great! Please bring it up to the dining room with some glasses, Miguel."

"Be right up, Robert! How wonderful and I missed it!"

Miguel carried the bottle of wine while his two men carried the glasses and some Portuguese cookies to celebrate.

When Miguel saw Mariah's happy tear-streaked face he ran to her and enveloped her in a hug and kissed her wet cheeks twice.

"My Mariah! I'm happy for you both!" Looking at Tony he exclaimed, "It's about time you claimed this prize! She is too good for you!" Miguel laughed when he saw Tony's shocked face.

"Only kidding, Tony. You are a prize yourself. Here, pour some wine for you and your soon to be wife. My men will pour for everyone else."

Raising his glass Miguel announced, "Let's drink to Mariah and Tony and many happy years together and lots of children too!" Miguel gave Tony the eye and winked. Miguel added, "Sorry about your arm,

Tony. You know who will wear the pants in your family!" Miguel laughed.

Tony let out a deep breath and sighed. "Thanks, I think, Miguel." Tony was wearing a smile now but still looked a little overwhelmed.

Everyone sat down at the table and sipped their port and tasted the delicious cookies made by Miguel. They had two things to celebrate – Sage was finally captured for good this time, and the engagement of Mariah and Tony. Things couldn't be more perfect right now. But not for everyone elsewhere.

***

Director Connor hung up the phone after speaking with Agent Bush and called for the FBI doctor to be brought immediately to the hospital to pick up the patient.

The four agents bundled up the patient and wheeled him out. It had begun to snow and they were concerned that the patient would get wet and cold. They couldn't afford to lose him now before he paid for his many horrendous deeds.

Arabella was in another patient's room and was not aware that Sherman was being taken out of his room. The doctor on call spoke to the agents and stopped them at the elevator inquiring, "Where do you think you are taking this patient?"

"We have orders from FBI Director Connor to take him to another facility for care. There is a doctor waiting in an ambulance downstairs. Please move out of the way. This is FBI business."

The doctor shrugged his shoulders and walked away. He didn't want to get involved. It wasn't even his patient.

The four agents went into the elevator and pressed the floor below that would take them to the waiting ambulance. As the door was closing Agent Bush met the eyes of Arabella, the nurse, as she tried to stop the elevator from closing.

Agent Bush kept his finger on the button to close the door and she finally had to give up as the elevator traveled downward. Arabella raced to the stairs to arrive at the main floor before they did.

The four agents pulled Sage out of the elevator and guided his bed to the ambulance as Arabella tried to grab the bed rail to hinder their progress.

One agent stepped in front of Arabella, gripped her arm and pulled it away. Arabella fought back and found herself in handcuffs as she was led away to a separate car with yet another agent.

She screamed out to Sherman, "I will come for you, Sherman!"

She sat in the FBI agent's vehicle as she helplessly watched the ambulance drive away. She hung her head and cried but dried her eyes on her sleeves after the agent took off her handcuffs and warned her to leave the premises or she would be arrested for obstruction of justice.

"I need to go back to work now. Can't I do that?"

"I will escort you back to your floor and will keep an eye on you. If you try to get in the way again, I promise you will be arrested."

Arabella shrugged and walked away. She had to think of what to do in order to get past this agent and find out where Sherman was taken.

After finishing her rounds of medications for the patients, Arabella stuck her head out of the last room and looked around for the FBI agent. He was nowhere in sight. She walked the long corridor, looked in both directions, and went back to the nurses' station. She asked one of the nurses if she had seen a large man walking the corridors in a black suit.

"No, sorry, never saw him. I started my shift about ten minutes ago. Why? What's going on?"

Arabella didn't answer for she was on the move again. She didn't know what she was going to do about finding Sherman but she would have to do some research into this man called Sage. Maybe then she would find out who his so-called niece is.

CHAPTER THIRTY-ONE

That night, at home, Arabella sat at her computer and put in "Sage and serial killers" hoping to find anything of interest. Arabella wasn't prepared to see so many pages of information on Sage.

She scanned through and read all this man's crimes that had crossed three states. She felt sick to her stomach over the graphic descriptions of the mutilations and rapes of the unfortunate young women. This was what the FBI agent had shared with her. She hadn't wanted to believe him.

She looked at the face of a younger Sage. His eyes were the same as Sherman, intense brown and wary. He wasn't handsome but was pleasant to look at...that's before the attack. Bad things happen to bad people, she thought. But, was this really her Sherman? He had to have changed. Sherman couldn't do those things, could he? Arabella had to know.

She looked over a curious caption, "Sage Copycat." *Hmm, what's this?* She read about a Professor Gyropolos who had killed two policemen and admitted killing a young woman in imitation of Sage's crimes.

The next item grabbed her attention. It was a photo of two women and a man who were responsible for putting Professor away. Professor had kidnapped the three and they somehow managed to get away. Under the photo were their names and an explanation that the woman, Mariah, had been in another situation a year ago with her Uncle Sage.

Arabella put in Mariah's name and received more information about her, her family, and her uncle's hospital. This is the place where Sage was finally captured, then escaped, but a short time later shot by Mariah.

Arabella wrote down the phone number for the hospital and formulated a plan of what to say when she called. Maybe she could find out where Sage went. His family may know. She wanted to talk to Mariah and find out why she shot her own uncle.

The following morning after breakfast Tony and Mariah prepared to go back home. Robert excused himself when his cell rang. Robert answered it. "Who is it, Dan? Okay, put her through."

Robert came back into the dining room and put the caller on speaker for all to hear.

"Yes, this is Robert Fontana, brother of Sage Fontana."

"My name is Arabella. I am the nurse who took care of your brother after the bear attack. I call him Sherman because I did not know his name all this time."

"Okay, but what can I do for you?"

"I got to know your brother and don't believe that he did what everyone is saying he did. I saw into his heart and he is a good man."

"You don't know what you are talking about, Arabella. You don't know Sage, the real Sage. He is evil and insane. He has done some horrendous things in his lifetime and needs to be punished."

"But he is your brother. He is your blood. You have to protect him and love you."

"No, he is not my blood. He was adopted. I will not protect him nor do I love him. I can't forgive him for trying to kill my family, those I hold dear. I will never forgive or forget what he tried to do."

"Is that how his niece feels too? She shot him three times?"

"Yes, I am sure that my niece feels the same as I do as well as my whole family. You would be better off to stay away from him."

"He is gone now. That is why I wanted to talk to you. I want to know where the FBI took him."

"I wasn't aware that he was being moved. I don't know where he is and even if I did know, I wouldn't tell you."

"I have to help him. I love him and he loves me too."

"I'm sorry but I can't help you. No one can help Sage now. He has to be put away for good. If he isn't, he will continue to come after my family. I will not allow that to happen again."

Mariah spoke up, "Don't get in the way, Arabella. If you interfere it could be the death of you too. Sage doesn't care for anyone but himself. Don't let him fool you."

"Is that you, Mariah? I read about you in the papers. You are quite famous, aren't you? Why did you shoot your uncle?"

"You don't know anything about what happened to Mariah, Arabella. There are few people who could have done what she did," Robert stressed.

"As to why I shot my uncle," Mariah interrupted angrily. "Sage killed my friend along with many other young innocent woman. I should have killed him and not just wounded him." Mariah shuddered as she took a deep breath.

"So you won't help me find Sage?"

"No, we will not, Arabella. You would be wise to forget about him. He cannot be saved by you or anyone else," Robert reiterated.

Mariah couldn't believe that Arabella was so naïve not to see through Sage. "I guess love is truly blind, in this case at least," she sighed.

"She sounds like a sad young woman," Beatrice observed.

"I only hope she will stay out of the way so Sage can be tried once and for all," Betsy stated.

Arabella had ended the call without saying goodbye and hung her head. It was clear that Sherman's family hated him and maybe they had a reason to if he tried to kill them.

She had to do something. She sat for a few minutes as an idea began to form in her head. It involved a 3D machine and a weapon.

***

Robert phoned Captain Kendall to report the call from Arabella. He didn't trust this woman. He felt she could in some way hinder the FBI from doing their job in putting Sage away.

"Thank you for calling, Doctor. I will check with the Director. I am sure he has things under control."

***

Sage didn't know where the agents were taking him. He knew that Arabella could no longer help him now that he wasn't at the hospital. Even if she promised to come get him, he knew that wasn't possible. He would have to find another way.

The four agents stayed by Sage's bedside per Director's orders. As soon as Sage was able they were to bring him into FBI headquarters. Director Connor wanted to begin proceedings to put this man away for good.

***

Captain Kendall called to check up on the patient but was told by the hospital that he had been moved. He quickly got in touch with Director Connor.

"Director, did you move Sage already?"

"Yes, I felt it was necessary. The nurse that was taking care of him was getting too chummy and interfering. She was trying to help him escape. We had to move him."

"I agree. I received a call from Dr. Fontana about this nurse. Evidently she bothered them about Sage's whereabouts. She claims that she is in love with Sage or Sherman, as she calls him, and that he loves her too. I'll keep an eye on her on my end. We don't want her getting in the way. There is no way that she will find Sage."

"We will make sure of that, Captain. He is being watched by four of my men. I will have him moved again tomorrow and then onto FBI headquarters. Thank you, Captain, for your assistance. We may be having that drink soon."

"Yes, I look forward to that day, Director."

CHAPTER THIRTY-TWO

The day finally came for Sage's trial. Mariah and her family were there to testify. Looking out into the seats Mariah spotted a woman all in white, possibly a nurse. Could it be Arabella? This woman was shooting daggers at Mariah. Arabella, thankfully, had not been able to interfere and now Sage would finally be on trial for his crimes. All the families of the murder victims of Sage's rage were there to see justice prevail.

Arabella followed Mariah and her family as they prepared to leave the courthouse. Sage was being escorted back to his cell after a full day of testimony against him. Arabella moved in front of Mariah and put her hand into her bag. Robert saw what was about to happen and stepped in front of Mariah.

What happened next was replayed by everyone in slow motion in their minds. Robert pushed Mariah aside and grabbed the gun from Arabella but not before it went off striking Sage in the head, killing him instantly, while he was sitting in a wheelchair, a short distance behind Mariah.

When Arabella realized what she had done she screamed, "Sherman, oh God Sherman! I didn't mean to hit you. I wanted to kill your niece for hurting you. I only wanted to help you. I love you, Sherman! I love you!" Arabella continued to rant and rave as the court officers took her away.

An ambulance was called but it was too late for Sage. They removed his restraints and took his body away.

Mariah held on tightly to her uncle to make sure he was not hurt. "Oh God, Uncle Robert! If you hadn't moved me away that woman would have killed me instead of Sage. How did you know she had a gun? And, how did she manage to bring it into the courtroom? Is this the woman, Arabella, who called you?"

"Yes, I guess it is. Who else would have tried something so crazy? I watched her face as she turned around and looked at you. When she reached inside her bag I knew she was going to do something. I couldn't wait to find out what. I reacted. The gun was not real. But real enough to harm someone. It was a plastic 3D copy from a machine. That's the reason she could bring it in. She must have put it together after she came into the courtroom."

"Thank God you did react, Robert!" Beatrice declared with relief as she hugged Mariah and Robert.

"Thank you, Robert!" Tony uttered in a voice choked with emotion as he stepped forward to shake Robert's hand but grabbed him into a tight hug instead.

Mariah hugged them both and noticed the tears in their eyes. She was shaking all over and crying herself. Mariah's parents joined in the group hug.

The police were inside and outside the courthouse and surrounded them as they prepared to take their statements as to what had happened.

It was finally over and Sage had escaped his imprisonment but would most likely rot in Hell.

***

Director Connor poured the first drink of scotch and raised his glass to Captain Kendall.

"Here's to us, Captain. It may not have ended the way we planned but Sage got what was due him. We also saved the state a lot of money not having to take care of his miserable life in prison."

"I guess you're right Director. But aren't you always?" Captain chuckled as he poured the second round.

***

Mariah had received an A+ as final grades in Journalism and Creative Writing courses from Ellie. She proudly stood up to receive her Bachelors of Arts degree and had already begun her great American novel. She was in no hurry to complete it. She was planning her wedding less than a month after graduation.

Betsy and Beatrice helped Mariah prepare for her special day. They were there to take her to the hairdresser's, and help her with her makeup and dress.

Now they both stood back to admire how beautiful she looked. They couldn't keep back the tears that filled their eyes as they blotted their makeup to keep it from smudging.

"Mom, Gram, you promised not to cry, at least not yet! You're going to make me cry! Here, have a sip of champagne. It's almost time!"

"Yes, dear," Betsy assented as she reached for a glass for her mother and herself. After taking a couple of sips they both took deep breaths.

"You look so beautiful, Mariah. I will do my best to keep the tears at bay but I can't promise anything. You take my breath away, honey. I am so proud of you. I love you!"

"I love you too, Mom. Thank you! I am a little nervous but I'm happy. I love him so much!"

"We know, dear. Tony loves you too. Now it's time for us to leave. You look extraordinary, sweetheart," Gram exclaimed.

"Thank you, Gram. I love you! Thank you for everything, for the ring, the house...," Mariah choked up.

"Now, don't ruin your makeup too. You already thanked me enough, Mariah. It gives me great pleasure to see you happy. I love you too. Mariah, I want to share some words with you from experience. Please humor this old woman."

"Of course, Gram. But I don't think of you as old."

"Thank you, Mariah." Gram sighed and continued, "Marriage is like a seesaw. There will be highs and lows. When you have highs, enjoy and embrace them. When you have lows, love one another fiercely and hold on tight for what goes down will come up again. Your grandfather and I were married nearly forty years, not long enough. I still miss him terribly. Cherish each day you have with each other. You will not know when it will be over."

"Oh, Gram. I'm sorry about Gramps, that you didn't have enough time together. I wish I could have met him. I will treasure your words of wisdom and remember them when we do have our ups and downs. Thank you!"

Mother and grandmother kissed Mariah and left to walk down the aisle before her.

The last year and a half had been stressful. The family hadn't really enjoyed or celebrated the holidays and now would make up for that with Sage finally gone and Professor Gyropolos in prison.

Tony stood anxiously waiting for the music to begin and his first glimpse of his soon to be wife. He thought over all that had transpired six months before. It was at last over and they could begin their lives together as husband and wife.

The weather was beautiful for early May and the air was clear and clean – perfect for a wedding, with Miguel as Tony's best man. Miguel left his two men in charge of the kitchen at the hospital so he could do his duty as best man and brought a new woman with him to the ceremony. He was definitely feeling happier than he had felt for a long time since he lost both his wife and daughter.

Ellie Jonas was Mariah's maid of honor. Mariah and Ellie had become quite close since the kidnapping episode.

Mariah's friend, Angie from college, was away in Europe studying and couldn't be there. Angie did send her good wishes to Mariah and Tony for much happiness in their life together. She promised to get together as soon as she returned in a month.

In attendance at the ceremony were Dr. Harper with his wife; Cara with her steady beau, Felipe; Laura with her date; and Dan with Sharynn, who was now wearing a ring of her own she and Dan had found at a pawn shop, a waterfall ring. Captain Kendall and Detectives Armano and Snyder were also in attendance. All were wearing smiles for a change.

Dan's backup, two new nurses, and a new doctor were left in charge of the patients and hospital making it possible for all regular staff to attend the ceremony. The new doctor was a woman who Robert had begun dating. It appeared that everyone finally had someone in their lives.

The music began and Tony looked up. He caught his breath as he saw Mariah all in cream floating down the aisle with her father on her right and her Uncle Robert on her left – the two other special men in her life.

Mariah hugged and kissed her father and uncle and smiled at her mother and grandmother in the front row before turning back toward her future husband. Tony beamed and took a deep breath and put his hand out to Mariah as she came to the altar to stand next to him.

Mariah felt a flutter inside her. She placed her hand protectively over her belly and smiled back at Tony. She had tested positive the day before. She would have a surprise wedding gift to give him later that night after they arrived in Bermuda for their honeymoon.

THE END

ABOUT THE AUTHOR

J. E. Spina is a retired administrative secretary from a public school system in Massachusetts. She has always loved writing poetry, novels and children's stories.

This is the third novel that J.E. Spina has published. She also has a short story collection written under J.E. Spina.

She has published ten children's stories and five middle-grade novels under Janice Spina. Janice is working on a YA series for girls and a YA fantasy.

Website: http://Jemsbooks.com
Twitter: http://twitter.com/janice_spina
FB Main Page: http://facebook.com/janice.spina.9
FB Author Page: http://facebook.com/janicespina7
FB Novelist Page: http://facebook.com/jespina7
Blog: http://Jemsbooks.wordpress.com

J.E. Spina lives in New Hampshire with her husband, John, and two tanks of fish. John is the illustrator of her children's books and designer of her book covers.

If you enjoyed this book, please leave a review where you purchased it and spread the word about it. J.E. Spina loves to hear from readers and welcomes reviews from all places that her books are purchased. She says, "It's like Christmas each time I receive a review!"

If you would like to be on J.E. Spina's email list to receive updates, newsletters, and special deals on books, please go to jjspina@myfairpoint.net and put in subject line **JEMSBOOKS MAILING LIST.**